Neighbourhood Watch

by **Anaïs Barbeau-Lavalette**

translated by **Rhonda Mullins**

Coach House Books, Toronto

First English-language edition. Originally published as *Je voudrais qu'on m'efface* by Éditions Hurtubise Inc., 2010.

Coach House Books acknowledges the financial support of the Government of Canada. We are also grateful for generous assistance for our publishing program from the Canada Council for the Arts and the Ontario Arts Council. Coach House Books also acknowledges the support of the Government of Canada through the Canada Book Fund.

LIBRARY AND ARCHIVES CANADA CATALOGUING IN PUBLICATION

Title: Neighbourhood watch / by Anaïs Barbeau-Lavalette ; translated by Rhonda Mullins.
Other titles: Je voudrais qu'on m'efface. English
Names: Barbeau-Lavalette, Anaïs, author. | Mullins, Rhonda, translator.
Description: Translation of: Je voudrais qu'on m'efface.
Identifiers: Canadiana (print) 2020036457X | Canadiana (ebook) 20200364618 | ISBN 9781552454176 (softcover) | ISBN 9781770566538 (EPUB) | ISBN 9781770566545 (PDF)
Classification: LCC PS8603.A705 J413 2020 | DCC C843/.6—dc23

Neighbourhood Watch is available as an ebook: ISBN 978 1 77056 653 8 (EPUB); 978 1 77056 654 5 (PDF)

Purchase of the print version of this book entitles you to a free digital copy. To claim your ebook of this title, please email sales@chbooks.com with proof of purchase. (Coach House Books reserves the right to terminate the free digital download offer at any time.)

To Geneviève, my little sister.
To Gilles Julien.

Author's Note

I first encountered the neighbourhood of Hochelaga-Maisonneuve through its children, thanks to its children.

After travelling around the world, a trip during which I trained my camera (I am a filmmaker) on some of the planet's fault lines – from people dying of AIDS in Soweto to street children in São Paulo – I searched for somewhere to help closer to home.

This is where I went. Toward this neighbourhood in eastern Montreal, one of the poorest in the country. Through the social pediatrician Gilles Julien, I was lucky enough to meet the person who would become my sister: Geneviève. I was twenty-one, and she was twelve. Holding Geneviève's hand, I got to know this neighbourhood and the people who live there. Going into their homes, in the midst of the collapse, I met little fighters, so full of life.

I had the good fortune to spend years working with them. Now they are adults, some still seem like an open wound, and others are miraculously full of light. This book is what I wanted to scream to draw attention so they would be heard.

To Geneviève, Kevin, and Eden, who inspired this book.

To Nathan, Geneviève's young son. From your proud godmother.

To all the little fighters in Hochelaga-Maisonneuve, and all the others around the world.

– Anaïs Barbeau-Lavalette

один

1

It's been dark in the stairway for a few lifetimes.

Light bulbs need changing, but everyone thinks someone else is going to do it. Eventually everyone just forgets that it's dark.

You sort of remember, only in winter, when you're tying your laces and trying not to fall.

Roxane has always had trouble with her laces. Two rabbit ears, that's what they say. But rabbit ears don't look like that.

Anyway, one day she's going to have boots and then fuck you, rabbits.

Roxane yanks her toque down on her head.

The pigeons are cooing in the ceiling. Roxane stops to listen.

If she were taller, she could peek between the boards to look at them. They must be settled in nicely, huddled together so they don't freeze. The dad, the mom, and the babies, all huddled up.

'Hi!'

Kevin's little voice. He's the neighbour in 62. When he talks, he flings his words. It's like they are going too fast for him, like they come out of his mouth and take off running. He's like that too. Uncontained. Right now he's trying to get his key in the lock, but he's so jumpy that it goes every which way but in the keyhole. Roxane watches him. There, it's in.

'Bye!'

He tears down the stairs.

He must be going to a match. He's been going to more ever since his mom took off. His father is Big, and Big always wins. Kevin wants to be like his father. He wants to win.

Roxane holds the handrail so she doesn't fall. She goes down slowly, looking at her feet.

On the next floor down, Mélissa throws opens the door to 58. Her bangs hide her eyes. It's as if she would rather stay hidden. The bangs are a compromise: I'm going, but you won't see my face.

Today is judgment day.

◆   ◆   ◆

Mélissa.

A virtually empty hearing room. Beige walls, brown benches. Wordless whispers in the air. Background noise with no substance, no personality. It's like everyone has worked hard to make it feel dead. Like they left life outside the door, waiting for this to pass: inside, it's just too rough to take.

From behind her bangs, Mélissa's eyes scan the few faces that have come to hear the decision. She doesn't know them. She can't grab on to any of them, even with just her eyes, even through her hair. There's her mother. But she's sitting at the other end.

Weathered. Even skinnier than last time. High as a kite.

She sits on the other side of the hearing room, hunched, shrunken. Her whole body says, 'Don't do this to me.' But Mélissa is the only one who hears it. Even though she is far away. She hears it. Because even hunched, even fucked up to her core, Meg is her mother. That's what the people here don't understand. Meg is her mother, no matter what.

It's probably just too simple.

Mélissa knows they put Meg at the other end on purpose so she can't grab her, hold on to her with her eyes, hold her tight.

Mélissa at one end, Meg at the other. Daughter, mother.

A few weary faces that feed on the decisions like a bad soap opera.

A tired judge takes three sentences to say that they won't be seeing each other anymore.

'Madame, you need to maintain a distance of fifty metres from your daughter until we have proof of your rehabilitation.'

Other empty words are threaded on the necklace, while Meg and Mélissa vanish a little more.

Kevin.

A church basement. Showy lights, strobe flashes, heavy metal.

Behind the smoke, a rough-looking crowd. Children, adults, excitement peaking.

'LET'S GO, BIG! KILL 'IM! KILL 'IM!'

In the middle of the room, a ring. Two wrestlers face to face, dressed in bright colours, faces distorted by grimaces and makeup.

In the crowd, Kevin, eyes glued to the match.

Smaller than the others, gets jostled but stays riveted to the ring, spellbound.

He gnaws on his lips, nervous.

The larger of the two wrestlers sends his adversary bouncing off the ropes, grabs him, throws him to the mat, jumps on him. The crowd goes wild. *Ding ding ding*. Big is declared the winner. The other guy is lying knocked out on the mat.

Kevin jumps for joy. 'Yessssssss!'

The winner, in a red cape, salutes the crowd in triumph. Shines under the white light.

'BIG! BIG! BIG!'

Kevin chants along with the crowd: 'BIG! BIG! BIG!'

His dad won again. When his dad wins, Kevin wins.

✦ ✦ ✦

Roxane.

Gets off the metro at Georges-Vanier. The Salvation Army is right across the street. She goes there often; she knows everyone there. The guys like her. They all say Marc is lucky to have a daughter like her.

'You're lucky, Marc. That's one special daughter you've got there.'

Roxane goes often. Not just because it's the only place in the world she's special. But because her father's been there a few months. Now he's done. Tonight he gets his certificate. That means he's won. He's still going to stay there until he finds a job and to make sure he won't backslide, but he's done, he's won, he's gone through all the steps. He's stopped drinking.

It's the fourth time he's dried out. The other times he fell off the wagon; he faltered. But the fourth time's the charm.

Roxane walks through the wall of smokers at the entrance. 'Hey, Louis. Hey, Pascal. Hey, Charles.' She goes inside. She feels good here. Everyone talks to her. Everyone thinks she's the best daughter in the world.

Her father is on the other side of the room, in a corner. Looks nervous.

The room is decorated with garland and lights. They're handing out free Cokes and coffee as you come in. Christmas is coming.

Her father got spruced up. Put on a blue shirt tucked into his pants. Slicked back his grey hair. Looks tired, his face weathered.

He spots her from across the room. Walks toward her. Long, unsteady strides. As if he might fall off his feet.

She's all he has left. You don't walk the same when you're walking toward the only thing you have left. He reaches her, finally, as if reaching the other side of the world.

'Hey.'

'Hey, Dad.'

Around them are others. Warriors. Some at the end of the battle, proud and restless. Others still making their first forays, a halo of alcohol as their shield.

Roxane takes her father's large hand in hers. They go sit on one of the benches set up in a row. At the front of the room, a mic and a Christmas tree the guys have trimmed. A few Christmas lights blink tentatively.

A man takes the mic. He is tall and pale, with all the panache of a basement in winter. His voice reverberates through the room.

'Tonight, we're going to celebrate winners. Big winners. For the new guys in the room, for those of you who are struggling and think you won't make it, the twelve guys you're about to see thought the same thing when they got here.'

Roxane looks at her father out of the corner of her eye. His aged face. His green eyes lost in the hollows. Turns toward her. Breaks into the remains of a smile.

The tired face of a survivor. She hugs him.

She's loved him for so long.

She wants to save him for good.

It's hot as hell in the room. And yet it's winter. There's something in here. A distillation of humanity. Guys, raw men.

'Our next winner's an old-timer ... He's fallen off the wagon a bunch of times. But now he's on it and holding strong ... Marc, come on up.'

Marc stands, unsteady.

'I'm going to ask his daughter, Roxane, to give him his certificate.'

Standing in front of a mic that's too short. A tank, a guy you'd picture at the throttle of a Harley, decked out in leather and tattoos.

But now he's standing in front of the guys, sunk into his shoulders. Trembling.

Emotion. He takes his time, because if he opens his mouth too fast he's going to cry too loud.

So he clears his throat.

Swallowing his tears, Marc tells the story of the end of the world that everyone in the room is familiar with, and the asshole you become at the end of that world. When your anchor is a goddamn brown bottle. When everything you are is contained in a few gulps, and your last breath is a burp. How it seems like you'll never get back on your feet. How you're hollow inside; how you've dug your own grave. Swallowed what was left of your pride. In over your head.

Marc grips the mic in his clammy hands. He has so little carapace left; he's so real it almost hurts.

In one breath to get to the end of it, he touches on Hell, the phone calls from his daughter – he looks at her – the phone calls from his daughter and her 'Don't give up, Dad,' the nights when he grabbed life by the scruff and bellowed whatever dreams he had left at it. His native Gaspésie, a wooden house at the edge of a cliff that plunges to the sea, a house all his own. Small – it doesn't have to be big – but on the ocean. And a motorcycle parked out front. To fly down the beautiful country roads. Free. With the wind in his face and his daughter on the back holding tight.

Dreams as a life preserver. So long as they are more solid than him.

Roxane hands him his certificate. She had come up with some words to say into the mic, but they aren't there anymore. She just wants to be his daughter, proud of him. She takes him in her arms. She feels so strong, and he, so little.

The family of warriors looking on applauds.

The doors open onto winter. On either side of them, there is a storm.

✦ ✦ ✦

A few streets away, the lights come back on in the church basement: the match is over. Sallow fluorescent lights on sunken faces. Back to reality. A lineup divides the space in two. Fat mothers, babies slung around their necks; broken-down old men, beer in hand; overexcited boys and crop-topped girls: everyone waiting their turn.

One by one, they climb into the ring and pose with Big.

The little kids wrap themselves in his cape. Big grabs them by the throat like a villain. 'Kill me! Kill me!' *Click*. The master of ceremonies snaps a Polaroid, and for five bucks, the kid leaves with a picture to hang on the wall. 'That's the time Big tried to kill me!'

It's Kevin's turn. He jumps in the ring, throws his arms around Big, who scoops him up, affection written all over his face. Kevin almost falls, steadies himself, poses seriously, pulling a bit of cape around his shoulders.

The master of ceremonies takes the picture and holds it out to Kevin.

'You're hooked there, Kev! You already got, like, twenty!'

'That's okay.'

✦ ✦ ✦

Roxane and Marc are sitting beside each other on their bench. The certificates have all been handed out. Now they drink coffee and try to convince themselves it will last. The night's winners mingle with the newly joined, hunched, frail, perforated from the inside, struggling to stand. In a year, it'll be their night, at least the ones who make it that far.

The guys are talking and laughing. The emotion hanging in the room gradually dissipates.

Roxane takes out a worn pack of Du Mauriers from her bag. 'From Mom.'

Marc grabs the old pack, the same as always. Inside there are twelve machine-rolled smokes. 'Thanks.'

Roxane rifles through her bag again. 'I brought you a gift.'

She takes out a shapeless object, messily wrapped in yellow tissue paper.

'What is it?'

'Open it.'

Marc's thick fingers touch the tissue paper. It's nice, a wrapped gift. Prolongs the surprise. The corners taped so it holds, so the surprise lasts. Marc lets the moment linger, touched. His callused fingers gently stroke the delicate paper, like a first meeting. Roxane could watch him do that her whole life.

The white triangle of a sail unfurls in his hand.

'A boat! It's beautiful ... '

'To remind you of Gaspésie.'

'Thanks. Thanks, sweetie ... I won't forget. I won't forget, promise.'

He wraps his strong arms around her.

You have to remember your dreams so you don't drown from within.

✦ ✦ ✦

It's dark out. It's snowing. The metro's going to stop running soon. In the entrance to the Salvation Army, the electric buzz of fluorescent lights.

Roxane puts her snowsuit back on. Marc, in an awkward gesture, adjusts her scarf. He would have liked to have been a father. A real one.

Sometimes he manages to tell himself that maybe it's not too late.

'Bye, sweetie.'

'Bye, Dad.'

'Get home safe. Take care of yourself.'

He says dad words, because he rarely gets the chance. They land a bit fake in the echoey entrance, but it feels good to say them.

'You too, Dad. Take care of yourself.'

'I'm proud of you …'

That one sounded true. Genuine dad.

'Me too, Dad, I'm proud of you …'

Marc hugs her again.

Roxane keeps her face buried in her father's neck, under his hair. That's where the warm smell of days spent without her accumulates.

✦ ✦ ✦

Dark silence in the apartment block. It's night. Even the pigeons are quiet. Only the wood of the stairs is expanding, echoing from wall to wall. A wisp of wind slips through the windows, seeking refuge between the floors, snaking under the doors.

A man suddenly splits the night and tears down the stairs, suitcase in hand.

A long furtive silhouette. In flight.

Mélissa is out like a shot, yelling after him. 'Where are you going?'

The man is already outside.

Mélissa yells louder. 'Where are you going?'

The man is already gone, and Mélissa's voice bounces off the walls.

In her pyjamas, in the stairwell, Mélissa doesn't cry.

Her stepfather is gone. Her mother too. She thought that if he loved Meg, he must love her a little too. Like an appendage to her mother. Too small probably. Too ugly.

Meg is gone, and her boyfriend too.

Frozen in the dark, Mélissa gets used to the emptiness. If she could leave her head there, she would.

The downstairs door opens again. The wind spots its chance. Wraps around Mélissa, who isn't moving.

The dull thud of laden feet on the steps. Roxane, coming up the stairs in a snowsuit, stops in front of her.

The girls look at each other. 'Save me,' they say silently to each other.

Mélissa tears herself away from Roxane's blue eyes and goes back inside.

два
2

Early morning. In number 61 of the apartment block, Roxane opens her eyes, looks at the alarm clock. Fuck. Up like a shot. She didn't wake her up. She's going to miss the bus. She's going to miss school. She's going to miss life.

Hurry.

Grabs the clothes on the floor. Yellow sweater, black jeans, two socks. Not matching, doesn't matter.

Hurry.

Kitchen. Opens the fridge, looks … Closes the fridge.

Her mother's bedroom, a sliver of light under the door.

'Mom?'

Louise, sleeping, frowns, pulls the covers over her head. Goddamn headache. Intense.

Back to sleep.

Roxane opens the curtains, lets a sunbeam into the grey room.

Louise pulls the covers over her head.

Tries to emerge. Can't.

Some of yesterday's smoke hangs in the air. Bits of sun get caught in it. Roxane too, for a second.

Beer bottles scattered on the floor. Counts them at a glance, fast. Eleven.

Her mother won't be getting up. Past eight beers, she doesn't get up.

Roxane picks up a few empty bottles, shoves them in her bag, and leaves the bedroom.

Under the covers, Louise holds her head in her hands.

✦ ✦ ✦

In number 64 of the apartment block, Mélissa opens her eyes and looks at her little-girl wallpaper. The same skinny princess in a purple dress that's too long, smiling a washed-out smile at a silly little fawn. The pathetic pair repeats itself all the way up to the ceiling. In six spots in her small bedroom, the princess is cut in half, giving her four eyes. It almost suits her better.

Tonight, Mélissa is moving into her mother's room. Because she won't be back, won't ever be back. She chose the street. Mélissa prays the winter is deadly cold. Deadly.

Mélissa is twelve, and starting now she has to give that little girl a kick in the ass. She has to pulverize her, she has to obliterate her. She has to be more adult than the adults, and she is totally fucking capable.

Yesterday, her stepfather fucked off. Had no one left to fuck, took off.

Just as well. Don't need him here.

Mélissa is twelve and totally fucking capable. More capable than anyone, even.

She gets up. The boys are already up and in the kitchen, plugged into the PlayStation. They suck up the flat light of the screen: their eyes are straws and their thirst is endless.

Mélissa feels grown-up. She unplugs the TV, cutting her little brothers off, and they start shouting: 'Not fair!' Mélissa puts music on the turntable. 50 Cent, full blast, fuck the neighbours. Fuck her little brothers. Fuck her stepfather. Fuck her mother. A little.

The boys are still shouting, but they're harder to hear over the music.

Mélissa gets dressed. So do they.

'Let's go.'

She grabs her things, their things, turns off the light.

Cold wind outside.

She breathes.

✦ ✦ ✦

Steve wakes up in front of the TV, streaks of makeup caked on his face. Cape around his neck, cigarette butt stuck to his face. He crashed right after the match. So tired.

Kevin is still asleep. This morning, women dressed in pink are stretching. 'And one, and two, let's go!'

Steve grabs the remote. POWER. Bye, ladies. Have fun.

Corner of the counter. Coffee. Cigarette. Tick-tock of the clock. Two cigarettes. 50 Cent's bass makes the walls and the little porcelain Dollarama figurines shake. Remains of his wife. As far as he's concerned, they can shatter.

Steve pushes the ashtray away. Puts a glass of orange juice on the table, a pill bottle beside it.

He stretches his back and goes to wake up his kid.

A blue bedroom. Star Wars wallpaper. Horror movies scattered on the floor. Drawings of wrestlers on the walls. Plush Spiderman, Batman, and Wolverine in Kevin's arms as he sleeps. Three knocks on the door.

'Get up, Kev!'

Silence.

Steve goes in, pulls on the covers. 'Come on, I gotta go.'

He leaves. Slams the door. He's gone.

Kevin gets up, turns on the computer, stretches, goes to pee.

Corner of the counter, he drinks the juice and swallows the Ritalin. His eyes sticky, he goes back to his bedroom and picks up his controller.

Kevin kills bad guys as he gets dressed.

◆　◆　◆

The sun is up on Rue Ontario, which is starting to come to life.

Meg's eyes are stinging, her feet are burning. She's shattered.

People are going to work. She's just finished.

She walks against the traffic on Rue Ontario, bumps into a guy who hates her for a couple of seconds and forgets her just as fast. Usually they like her a little before chucking her aside. Makes for a change.

She counts her cash as she walks. Ten clients. A good night.

Store windows go by. White beds with thick duvets, dry aquariums with plastic plants, the laundromat with its sleeping washing machines, where the lonely seek each other out to pair their unpaired socks. At this hour, the stores have no personality. Empty, they're waiting. Still frames resting until they're put to use again. Like Meg in the morning.

Meg likes this brief moment in the day when she stops being an invitation.

The snow squeaks under her heels, absorbing the weight of her footsteps. The wind is at her back. It's on her side. It feels good.

From an anonymous alley, Meg heads into her room. Her cave.

It's cold. She undresses under the covers, curls up. Sighs.

Her big made-up eyes go out for the day.

✦ ✦ ✦

'C'mon, guys. We're going to be really late!'

The boys stop at every decorated balcony. Every morning, Mélissa takes them down a different street. Today, it's Rue Davidson. So far, it's the best: almost all the houses are decorated.

The Christmas lights climb high up, winding around staircases and blinking their whole length. It's pretty.

At the corner of Rue Adam, there's an inflatable Santa gyrating, blown up from the inside. He suddenly bends forward, then suddenly bends back, his back broken. Then he starts over. The boys think it's funny. It's like Santa's going to throw up.

Walking makes a *squeak squeak* sound. The snow is alive and screams with every footstep. A hurried *squeak squeak* balcony to balcony. The wind sounds cold too. It has escaped from its bottle, takes off laughing because no one is freer than it.

Some people are so jealous of the wind, they kill themselves. That's why more people die in winter.

'Look out!'

The guy from the depanneur is weaving on his bike with empty cases of beer. Almost ran into them.

'Hey, Santa! Where'd you get your licence, fuck's sake?' Mélissa calls out to him.

Because now it's up to her to protect her little brothers.

They're getting closer to the prostitutes on the street corner. There are always two or three left, even at this hour. They must be freezing, toes crammed in their pointy shoes. Mélissa doesn't even feel sorry for them. She grabs the boys by the hand and takes a deep breath. She walks by them. Looks without looking. If her mother were there, she would recognize her right away. Even without looking, she would recognize her. Even if she were hiding, she would recognize her. Some things there are no words for. Some things you can't explain. Close up or far away, blind or dead, if her mother is nearby, Mélissa feels it in her body. And that morning, she's not there.

Feeling lighter, Mélissa walks to school without talking.

✦   ✦   ✦

Standing tall on the stoop of the apartment block, Roxanne waits. She likes being outside better than being inside, even when it's cold. She swallows air and tries to make rings with the winter vapour that comes out of her mouth. It works.

In the street, the neighbour is clearing the snow from his car with a broom.

The yellow school bus is at the end of the street.

Roxane still takes it even though she's too old. Her mother, the social worker, the school, the principal, everyone decided for her.

She could walk, she told them. 'It's not far. I could walk.'

She could take the regular bus too. But they don't want her to. They're afraid.

Plus, the yellow bus is free for dummies. If it's free …

'Sorry!'

Kevin bumps into her as he runs by and rushes into the street. He runs to the end of it and disappears around the corner.

The yellow bus stops in front of Roxane. From the stoop, she looks off into the distance, as if the bus weren't here for her. 'Who, me? You came to get me?' As if it had the wrong girl. She doesn't keep it up long, because pretty soon the bus starts honking.

She goes down the steps. One, two, three. Climbs the other steps. One, two, three. The lady says the same hi as every other day, and Roxane doesn't answer.

She heads through the bus, which is so long. Walks through it like it's a hospital corridor under fluorescent lights. She doesn't want to see the other dummies. They're gross. She sits beside a guy in a wheelchair. He's all strapped in, attached so he doesn't roll away when they take a corner. Everyone on the bus is crazy. They can't talk or they can't walk. They drool. They stink.

The bus drives around Hochelaga picking up trash.

Roxane looks out the window. She's not a dummy. She's not like other kids, but she's not a dummy.

Socially maladjusted. That's her label.

They didn't say whether there's a cure, or whether it's catching.

The bus stops in front of the school. She gets off, fast. Always first.

She crosses the street to the depanneur.

✦　✦　✦

At the depanneur counter, a few bodies waking up. Men and women, hunched so they can't see too far ahead. They got their cheque, and they're lining up to scratch for a million. Straightening up a little, they can see they haven't won. But for just a second before seeing the result, the second when they picture another life for themselves somewhere in the sun or in someone's loving arms, just to savour that moment before the 'Better luck next time!' they line up, they pay, and they scratch for a glimpse of promise in the day-to-day slush.

Roxane takes the empty beer bottles out of her bag, puts them on the dep guy's counter, and he counts them at a glance. 'Ninety cents,' he says.

Roxane gets a May West. Her eyes meet Mélissa's, the neighbour with the snot-nosed little brothers stuck to her like glue, their noses in a bag of chips, in a salty hole. If they could burrow their entire bodies in it, they would. Roxane looks at Mélissa hiding behind her overgrown bangs and thinks she's no better off, because her mom's a prostitute.

'Hi!'

'Hi!'

Roxane exchanges her beer bottles for a May West, and for two seconds considers herself lucky.

◆ ◆ ◆

The bell has rung. Kevin is lined up in the schoolyard. All the other kids are at least two heads taller than him. He would give his PlayStation to grow a bit more, particularly when he's lined up. It's cold, but the teachers leave them standing around in the schoolyard before going in so they're in order, so they're properly lined up.

Kevin gets whacked in the back of the head. He turns around. Laughter erupts from the lineup. Kevin pulls his toque down on his head, turns again to see who hit him. Chews on his lip. Gets hit a second time. Harder this time. Bites his lip, ouch, ouch, ouch in his head. Tears well up. Don't start crying, you poof. Kevin doesn't turn around and this time hopes with all his heart that the line will move move move … His toque flies to the back of the line. It's like everyone is laughing, everyone is doubled over. 'Go on! Go get your hat, headcase!' 'Not moving anymore?' 'Put your pill in the wrong hole?' They're laughing hard. Kevin walks back along the line, staring as far into the distance as he can. His lip is bleeding, he's holding back tears – the line is long, endless. At the very end, a hand holds out his toque. It's Roxane, the one who talks to herself. He grabs it from her and jams it on his head. That's when they decide to get the line moving.

◆ ◆ ◆

Roxane walks against the flow in the hallway. Just like in life. Everyone is heading to class, rushing in the other direction. She weaves her way toward the library at the other end of the hall. At her desk, Ms. Bilodeau barely lifts her head, pretending to read the dictionary. Ms. Bilodeau stalls at the letter L because she is dreaming of Love.

'Hello, Roxane.'

Every morning, Roxane goes by the library. She knows that Ms. Bilodeau is hiding a Harlequin romance behind her dictionary. 'Because anything is still possible within these pages,' she explained to Roxane one day, visibly moved.

The principal isn't romantic, so Ms. Bilodeau pretends to read the dictionary during busy periods.

'Hi, Ms. Bilodeau.'

Roxane walks past her, heads toward the aisle. Her aisle. The one that says 'World.' She walks back and forth a few times, dragging her index finger over the spines of the books that are sticking out. She likes the sound. A gentle sound, like a caress. She stops finally at the Rs.

R, as in Russia.

She's looked through all the books on Russia. More than once, even. This time, she chooses the big red book. The pictures are in colour, and there is Russian vocabulary at the end. She already knows a few words. *Snieg* means snow, *oblako* means clouds, *zima* means winter, *louna* means …

The second bell rings. Time for class.

Roxane hugs the red book to her chest and heads to the counter.

Ms. Bilodeau records the book. Stamps the card. 'Two weeks,' she says.

Roxane's eyes skim the yellowed pages of the romance novel, poorly hidden behind the dictionary. To each her own journey. Roxane puts the book in her bag and leaves.

'Hey, dumdum, you're on the wrong floor!'

Laughter.

The library is on the floor for regular classes. They know how to read. Roxane goes back down to her class, one floor down. To sixth grade for mental cases.

✦ ✦ ✦

Today they're making a nativity scene out of modelling clay.

Kevin hands out images of Jesus's family, with the sheep, the grey donkey, and the rest of the gang.

On her desk, Mélissa draws Mary from the pile. She is dressed all in white. Her hands are long and folded over each other.

'I want to do her.'

'Me too.'

Mélissa and Roxane root through the jars of modelling clay.

'There's no white.'

'Fuck. There's no white.'

'Miss? There's no white for the Blessed Virgin!'

'Then choose another colour, girls.'

They choose red. The modelling clay smells like fruit punch.

Roxane makes a head. Mélissa a body.

'She needs boobs.'

'Yeah, big boobs!'

Each girl rolls a ball in the palm of her hand. Mélissa's ball is bigger than Roxane's, so Roxane adds a little modelling clay till Mary's boobs are even. Mélissa sticks them above the stomach and adds a lemon nipple to each one.

Roxane makes a yellow veil, while Mélissa fashions a long butt crack. There. The girls assess their work. It's like a mini-snowwoman with big fruit-punch boobs and lemon nipples.

The girls want to eat Mary because she smells so good. Mélissa bites off her head. Surprised, Roxane starts laughing and bites off her legs. Marie is legless and decapitated: the girls are doubled over laughing. Their teeth full of modelling clay, they are sent out into the hall.

◆　◆　◆

Louise gets up and sits in front of the TV. Women are cooking. A meat dish, something with apricots. In her bathrobe, Louise rolls cigarettes one after the other while they roll out pie crust, talking about the resurgence of tourism in Cuba. Eyes staring into space, fingers on the roller. Goddamn headache. She takes a swig of Coke.

'Stuff the apricots in the holes.'

She lights a cigarette.

Louise, alone and small in the dirty white living room. Her feet in old Fred Caillou slippers. She sniffs.

'Then mince the garlic.'

10:20. Recess. Louise thinks of Roxane. She must be playing outside. With her friends. Maybe. Outside with her friends.

Louise stubs out her cigarette, pulls up the covers, and curls up on the sofa in a little ball. For a moment, she tries to remember her daughter's laugh. The way it erupts. A laugh all her own.

'Put the meat pie in the oven at 350° and …' Shut up. She turns off the TV.

Closes her eyes. She falls asleep, her hands on her head.

✦ ✦ ✦

Kathy and Kelly.

A body rolled up in fabric underneath winter.

'I'd almost like to be a tourtière!'

A raspy voice, amused, hiding under thick layers of clothes.

A square of cardboard set in front of a pawnshop. In the window, presiding over the other objects for sale, a display of televisions is precariously balanced. All the screens show a tourtière baking in the oven.

'Hey, Kelly. D'you get it? I'd almost like to be a tourtière! Check it out, it looks nice and toasty!'

On the street corner, Kelly watches the cars like a cat on the prowl, squeegee in hand and claws extended.

Around Kathy, the dogs doze, frozen. Kathy shakes the cold, empty beer mug; not one penny this morning. And yet normally when it's cold …

She looks up at the tourtières in the pawnshop window. Forgets where she is, can almost smell the cinnamon coming from the TVs, the crust darkened by the browned butter, the little squares of wet potatoes and ground meat still a little pink.

Kelly joins Kathy on the cardboard square, the two forms become one; the dogs slip under the covers with them. Kathy and Kelly curl up in each other's arms, suddenly richer than the rich.

From the other side of the street, all that can be seen is a pile of fabric in front of Madame Taillefer's fifteen pink kitchens. On the ground, an empty metal mug.

+ + +

Outside, plump snowflakes are falling. Roxane is sitting at the back of the class, looking out the window. The teacher is dealing with an outburst at the front. The kid is on the floor, and he's yelling, scrambling in every direction. 'Calm down, Kevin, calm down.' The teacher tries to restrain him. It's been happening a lot since his mother left. The social worker should show up any minute now for a time out, then things will get back to normal, as if nothing ever happened. A time out is a technique they learn at social worker school. It's like a wrestling hold for children. With arms and feet pinned, there's just the yelling to deal with, but when the kid can't move, he quiets down on his own.

Roxane watches the snow falling. The snowflakes look soft, but really, they're cold. Lots of things are like that, she thinks.

Whenever something sort of serious happens, Roxane looks outside. If it goes on too long, she leaves for Russia.

She opens the big red book on her desk. Round castles that look like macarons. They're so beautiful they don't look real. She reads: 'The Krem-lin.' The sun hangs overhead, bits of light that shine so bright she wants to collect them. She would like to gather them up, put them in a box, and hide the box under her pillow. Roxane turns the page. There's a woman with a red scarf on her head. Tendrils of hair stick out from under it. Blond. Soft.

'Anastasia is a young Moscovite.' It's written underneath.

Anastasia has red cheeks and black eyes that look straight on.

They're steady. It's like they know everything and it's not even that bad. It's like they're saying, 'It's okay, it's okay.'

Roxane looks at Anastasia, their eyes meet, for a long time.

+ + +

A short break between clients. Meg is squatting at the end of an alley. Peeing. A thin stream that trickles to the middle of the alley, forges its own path, not giving a shit about obstacles. A thin stream that couldn't give a shit.

Meg stands up, legs bare. Pulls up her nylons.

There's a run. Fuck, there's a run.

Whatever. Anyway, they know we have runs, Meg. You think they come here to fuck Miss Universe?

Meg silently talks to herself and smiles. She pulls up her run over all the other ones, which are invisible.

They have runs too.

She slips in her shoes.

We're all full of fucking runs.

With all her runs, Meg reaches the street, following the course of her stream as it disappears into the gutter.

◆　◆　◆

Roxane comes home from school.

Heavy backpack.

Frozen door, broken doorbell.

Rings once. Twice.

Goes in by the back.

Roxane barely knows the days of the week, but she knows when it's cheque day. It's today. There are one two three beers on the counter. The TV is on loud. Too loud. Her mother is drinking in the living room.

A swig. A soggy hello. Roxane, eyes worried, searches to see what's left of her mother.

Dark circles under eyes, holes in her smile, grey bathrobe open, showing her wrinkled neck, suffering slouched on the sofa.

'Hi, Mom.'

Silence.

Her mother looking at the TV. Roxane looking at her mother. Roxane wants her to look at her. She wants her to see her before he gets home. Because once he gets home, the house is on fire and it's too late. The TV as a shield, Louise doesn't have the guts to look at her.

It's a quarter to six. Roxane doesn't have time to hope. She goes into her bedroom. It's dark in there. It's cold in there. She sits looking out the window. In the distance, she can spot the river. Snow is falling on it. White lines from the sky to the ground, long, long, never-ending. 'Snow … *Sni-eg* … ' Between her deserted lips: '*Snieg*.'

The sound of keys. Then the door. He's home. The shouting's going to start.

Red numbers on the alarm clock: 6:00.

Head under the pillow.

+ + +

Night falls suddenly, as if, starting now, there were something to hide.

At the pawnshop, they've rearranged the TVs, stacked them in the shape of a Christmas tree. A festive idea. A concept. The same image repeats on each screen. A woman, black veil on her head, cries, looking up at the sky. A child in her arms. Dead, no doubt. The same woman, the same child, on twelve screens in the pawnshop window. On twelve screens that together form a pathetic excuse for a Christmas tree. Night might as well fall all at once.

Kelly and Kathy watch. The woman the woman the woman the woman the woman the child the child the child the child the child the child.

It's snowing now on Rue Ontario. Wet feet are hunting for gifts. Kathy rolls a joint.

+ + +

A storm hangs over the apartment. Roxane has time. She slips into the kitchen. She looks for something, head in the fridge. She's hungry.

'Rox!'

She jumps. Her mother is calling her. 'Roooxxxx!'

Get back to the bedroom. Fast.

Louise in the living room, bottle in her mouth, him beside her, smoking in silence.

'Have you done your homework?'

Don't want to talk to you, she says in her head. Don't want to. Don't want to. Don't want to.

Get back to the bedroom. Fast.

'Hey! Talk to your mother, for chrissake.'

'C'mon, Mom ...'

'You don't want to talk to me?'

Her voice is dribbling.

'...'

'Well, go ahead, dammit ... Go rot in your room.'

'Shut up, Louise!'

Him, spewing smoke. Gets her in line. Bridled like a horse. Roxane knows it's starting. That's how it begins. Her bedroom. Fast. Each stride as long as the world. One voice rising and biting, the other voice starts overtop of it, the words thick, it shoots, it spits, it spews venom. Roxane in her bedroom the window the snowflakes *snieg snieg*.

'You're a fucking idiot.'

'Fuck you!'

A dull thud. She hits him.

Roxane vanishes, dives into another place, far, as far away as possible.

'You sonofabitch.'

'Don't you touch me!'

Snieg. Snowflakes like long white lines in the sky that fall and fall and fall.

'You want to kill me, huh?'

She laughs.

'Shut up!'

She shouts.

Knock at the door.

Snieg. It's pretty it's pretty it's pretty. 'Open this door, Roxane, goddammit ...' Long lines long lines. Bang! The door forced in, Louise in front of the window, Louise in her bedroom, in front of the snow that keeps falling.

'Look at the snowflakes, Mom,' she might have said, and then, 'Oh yes, they're pretty.'

'Jesus! You just run away? I'm in shit, and you're nowhere to be seen …'

Her words drag along the ground, hot air pours out through the gaps in her mouth.

'C'mon, Mom.'

'Goddammit!'

Louise falls. Roxane grabs her arm.

'Get up, Mom.'

She grabs her by the waist. Louise is crying.

He comes in, drags her by the T-shirt. 'That's enough of this crap, for chrissake.'

He lifts her up. It's tight around her neck.

'It's tight around her neck,' Roxane says, quietly.

Louise is yelling.

'It's tight around her neck,' Roxane says again.

He drags her out of the bedroom.

Silence.

Roxane closes her door. Screaming. Screaming. Words. Blows. Her name. Her mother screaming her name. Roxane opens her drawer. Looks for her headphones, finds her headphones.

Shostakovich, violins. Louder, louder still. The violins the window the snow *snieg* that falls like lines from the sky to the water like vines she could grab on to, to rise so high, all the way up, the snowflakes fall in vines from the ground to the sky, Shostakovich's violin flows over her, then flows in her. Roxane is a string, shrill under the bow, Roxane vibrates, Roxane explodes, flies over the street, over the dead bodies, over the shit, to the boats, to the river, to Russia. Roxane is a symphony.

три
3

Morning breaks. The cathode-ray window of the pawnshop is still dormant, screens sleeping on a hypnotic storm. Sailing through winter on their square of cardboard, the hump of Kathy's and Kelly's bodies contorts in the morning. A soft voice glides over them.

'You wouldn't have a cigarette, would you?'

Meg's long legs with runs split the morning horizon.

Sleepy, Kelly jams her hand into the maze of fabric that makes up her shell. At the innermost layer, next to the heat of her body and safe from thieves, Kelly finds a cigarette, which she offers with her broken fingers to the tired prostitute.

'Thanks.'

✦ ✦ ✦

They are laughing at nothing, all together, as if someone had said, 'When I say go, everyone laugh.' They are all laughing, even though you don't get the joke, as if they are laughing at you behind your back. Stupid morning radio. Mélissa swats the radio. It doesn't turn off.

Mélissa gets up. It's dark in the kitchen. The stepdad hasn't come back. There's no sign of him, no beer, no cigarette butts, no nothing. He won't be back. This time, it's for real.

Mélissa opens the fridge. She grabs the orange juice container and takes a swig: she spits. It tastes like vomit. She surveys what's left. Salad dressing, tomato sauce, mayo, relish, ketchup, chocolate sauce. Mélissa squirts a shot in her mouth. She opens the freezer and empties the contents onto the table.

'What are you doing, Mélissa?'

The boys in pyjamas, still sleepy.

'I'm getting organized.'

◆ ◆ ◆

There's frost on the windows, lines criss-crossing to create a curtain inside and out. As if winter had fingers that could draw.

Roxane is tired.

Louise is sleeping on the sofa. Roxane approaches, bends over her face. An inch from her skin. She runs her eyes over her. Lingers at the pits, marks, lines. A trail of drool along her cheek. Beer drool. Runs a long finger over it – her mother's drool – and traces the line up to her mouth. Open. Dry. Dead.

If only she would die.

Roxane picks up seven empty beer bottles from the floor and takes off.

Outside, Roxane walks, her head held high. She didn't take the yellow school bus. They can eat shit. She will find her own way, she will go to school like a normal girl. Totally normal.

I think I have to turn here. I think this is where I have to turn. The yellow school bus turns here. I think ...

The street name is there, but it takes a long time to read. Reading takes a long time. She reads slowly, and anyway, she doesn't know what street she should take, so even if she knew the name ...

Never been this way. I think. Don't recognize it, don't recognize anything. Go back.

Roxane retraces her steps. Running. Turns the corner, goes back to the start, goes back to the front of her apartment block. One, two, three. Goes up on the stoop. Roxane is out of breath. They were right.

The yellow school bus is coming down the street. One, two, three. Roxane gets in without even pretending it's not coming for her.

They were right. Roxane is mental.

◆ ◆ ◆

At the depanneur across from the school, Mélissa haggles with the owner for a package of salty noodles, the boys hanging from her sleeves.

'I'll pay you next time, c'mon. I'm here every morning!'

Roxane goes in, takes the empty beer bottles from her bag, puts them on the counter.

A look from Mélissa, a quick count.

'Can you give me two?'

'Huh?'

'Bottles, can you give me two? I don't have enough cash.'

Roxane looks at Mélissa and the two snot-nosed kids hanging from her. Looks at the dep owner, who is waiting, a pack of salty noodles in hand.

'Yeah. I'll give you two.'

Mélissa pushes two empty bottles in the dep owner's face, grabs the pack of noodles from his hands – 'Let's go, guys!' – and tears out of the store.

Roxane knows it takes seven empty bottles for a May West. She has five left. She leaves.

Mélissa is already way ahead, almost at school. She walks, head down so the cold doesn't hit her face. The boys get behind her to shield themselves from the wind. Mélissa slices through the air for them. She creates a slipstream for them like geese. Mélissa is a warrior.

Roxane thinks she's beautiful.

◆　◆　◆

Steve is lying on his back, legs apart, under a rusted Peugeot. His blackened hands roam its metallic guts as his expert eye spots the crack, which he seals mechanically. Last Christmas, he gave Kevin a model of this car. A small silver Peugeot, nice and clean. In a nice box. They assembled it together, spent all night on it. It made the kid happy.

Steve sings 'Blue Moon' under the rusted Peugeot. The day is ending, and he has done a good job. Even though he doesn't have a car himself, there are a few of them still roaming the city because of his skill.

A deep voice resonates above the car.

'Steve! Boss wants to see you!'

Bad feeling. Steve doesn't move, holed up in his rusted metal burrow.

'Hey, Wrestlemania. Let's go.'

Steve emerges from the shadows. Wipes his hands.

✦ ✦ ✦

At the back of Garage Lacombe, a few employees, faces blackened by sludge, watch the scene, immobile. Steve grips a rag in his hands, the black oil dribbles onto the floor.

'Jesus, why? What is this shit?'

'The garage isn't making enough money. We have to let people go. That's how it is, Steve, I – '

BANG!

The boss's face smashed into the dash. Steve mashes the rag into his cheek – the oil runs into the boss's mouth. Steve kicks the door and takes off.

On Ontario, a guy in the crowd. In his pockets, blackened hands, balled in a fist. He's all alone and he wants to cry.

Roxane is immersed in her book. A large public square. People look like they're walking fast, the way they do here. They look down at the ground and keep moving. Only the pigeons are still in the midst of hurried steps. The pigeons are restful. They leave tracks on the ground like little stars. The people rushing by trample the stars.

Roxane lifts her head, looks outside.

The children are playing in the schoolyard, in their snowsuits, like cosmonauts. It's like they're floating. It snowed. The day is calm. The air is white and damp.

The lights flicker in the classroom. The teacher has just come in.

Roxane looks for the page she folded at the corner. Anastasia. Reassuring eyes looking back at her.

◆ ◆ ◆

There's a test. She didn't know or forgot. She doesn't understand the questions. AT ALL. Like they're written in another language.

She puts her head down on her desk. Anastasia looks at her.

'Roxane?'

She jumps.

The teacher is standing beside her.

'Are you working?'

' … Yes.'

'You haven't started yet?'

' … '

'Do you understand?'

' … '

'You have to complete the sentences with the words "I," "you," or "we."'

'Yes.'

Understand nothing nothing nothing.

'Okay?'

'Yes.'

The teacher looks at the picture of Anastasia. 'Russia again. She's pretty, isn't she?'

'…'

'She looks a bit like you, don't you think?'

Roxane looks at Anastasia. Yes. She looks like her. It's true. She looks like her. '… Yes.'

Roxane is excited. Finally she looks like someone.

The teacher closes the red book. 'Concentrate, dear. Make an effort. You have to understand your own language before you learn others, don't you think?'

'…'

◆ ◆ ◆

The TV pyramid shows winter scenes. Live. Kelly and Kathy, under their mountain of fabric, are huddled between their dogs, only their eyes sticking out. Two pairs of sea-blue eyes in the grey-white of Rue Ontario. Survivors that the winter meteors avoid at the last minute.

'Death by snowplow is a heroic death.'

'Any death is heroic.'

'Then we're all heroes?'

'Yep.'

'Me in particular.'

'Me in particular!'

They kiss as they await death. Mouths are warm. A lover's tongue is reassuring.

'Hey!'

A guy's voice, a metallic voice.

He's standing, backlit, splitting the street in two. They don't see his glassy eyes. They don't see his fists balled in his pockets. But they figure it out because of the bitter cold that settles deep inside them.

Kelly speaks in what she hopes is a steady voice. 'Don't worry, man. We'll pay you in – '

A kick to the face. Kelly's nose cracks, broken, starts bleeding, while the dogs start barking.

'Fucking psycho!'

Kathy covers Kelly with her body. A flimsy human shield. The guy spits on them. In the language of the street, that means they're done talking. He wants money. He walks away, leaving the perfect promise of his imminent return.

With the end of her sleeve, Kathy tries to soak up the blood streaming from Kelly's nose. They don't say anything, because there is nothing to say.

Like a rock in the middle of a torrent, the two bodies entwined under a pile of fabric.

The day goes by, but the cold remains.

They should go somewhere far away, but this is their home. This piece of cardboard is their country. Everywhere is nowhere, except here.

Kelly and Kathy slowly go to sleep. The dogs stand guard.

◆　◆　◆

In her bedroom, Roxane is reading under the covers. By flashlight, so they forget she's there. Beside Anastasia's picture, a block of text:

'With its e-nor-mous land mass, Russia is home to a va-ri-e-ty of races, and the stan-dard for fe-mi-nine beau-ty va-ries wide-ly. How-ev-er, there are cha-rac-ter-is-tic traits, such as pale skin, grey-blue eyes, blond or chest-nut hair, plump-ness from lack of ex-er-cise and the se-clu-sion de-mand-ed by win-ters that last seven or eight months. With their pale faces, their de-li-cate fea-tures are some-what fa-ded like the fea-tures of the face of the moon, and these blur-ry lines make for faces with a Nor-dic soft-ness and nor-thern grace.'

◆　◆　◆

'Jesus, it's cold!'

Meg hops leg to leg, faster and faster. She stumbles, almost falls. The girls smile, Meg too. She's lost a tooth; there's a big gap right in the middle. She couldn't care less. She laughs anyway; it warms her up.

From the corner of the sidewalk, Mélissa spots her at a distance. She's there, laughing hysterically. Her mother, laughing with the other girls.

Night falls. Their day is starting. Fishnets. She must be freezing to death.

Mélissa slows her step. She wants to see her. She wants to be seen.

On the other side of the street, Mélissa stops across from the group of prostitutes.

One of the girls notices her, taps Meg's shoulder.

'One of yours, Meg.'

Meg stops laughing and turns toward Mélissa.

'Fuck.'

Meg looks down at the ground.

Her mother's 'Fuck' crosses the street and slaps Mélissa in the face. Two sketches of women, frozen, facing each other. Trying to find each other.

Slowly, like a mountain climber, as if she were scaling a slippery slope, Meg raises her eyes to her daughter.

Eyes forming a bridge from one to the other, from either side of the sidewalk, they look at each other. Fuck the fifty metres, fuck. Suspended above the world, for another moment, they look at each other. Mélissa is warm. It's been a long time.

Meg gently places her hand on her neck.

From the other side, Mélissa watches the maternal gesture. Tries to decipher it. *Cover your neck.* She's saying *cover your neck.* Definitely, that's what she means, *cover your neck, you're going to freeze.* Mélissa pulls her coat up over her bare skin.

A car goes by and cuts the bridge in two.

◆ ◆ ◆

'Sure is quiet next door! Bet they drank their pay last night, eh, Dad?'

The TV is on in the little apartment. The TV people are talking over each other, all jumbled. Steve is crashed on the sofa in the living room smoking, staring into space. He doesn't answer. In the kitchen, Kevin empties the jar of relish on his hot dog.

'Aren't you gonna get ready?'

He yells over the voices. Steve doesn't hear him. Kevin takes a bite.

'Dad, aren't you gonna get ready?'

On the sofa, Steve rouses from his stupor. 'Mmm.'

Takes a drag of his cigarette. A long one to impress his kid. It burns halfway down.

'Whoa!' Kevin says, feigning admiration.

Steve blows smoke in his face, smiling from the corner of his mouth. 'Wipe your face. You got relish everywhere.'

Kevin wipes his chin on his sleeve.

'Jesus, Kevin! Use a dishcloth, for chrissake. You're not a three-year-old.'

Kevin is surprised by his father's tone.

Looks at him a moment, frozen. Then heads to the kitchen to grab a dishcloth.

+ + +

On the other side of the wall, the little brothers are watching *Black Vampire*. They've already seen it three times, but they never get tired of being scared. Mélissa plopped them in front of the screen after playing mother. What she can remember of it. Someone who is there at home, and who appears when you need something. Like when you're hungry or you're smelly and it's bath time. She poured bowls of cereal with banana slices. She even put chocolate syrup on top to make her little brothers happy. So they'd like it. But the chocolate sank to the bottom, and they didn't even see it. Didn't taste it. It's not easy being a mother. Maybe that's partly why hers left. Because Mélissa couldn't taste her effort.

Now Mélissa is tired. Inside, it's all tired. Doesn't want to do anything else.

Her mother's bedroom is too big with no one in it. The window looks out over the alley.

It's snowing outside. Around the street light, it's like a puddle of light stuck to the sky. There's a squirrel balancing on a wire, and a few sparrows waiting. Behind them, the sluggish river, ice its shield.

Mélissa smacks the window. The squirrel doesn't fall, and the sparrows are still there. She smacks it again, harder. Still nothing. Nothing is moving; it's like she doesn't exist.

Mélissa turns out the light and slips into the big bed. It smells like her mother's hair. She falls asleep.

✦ ✦ ✦

Steve has closed the bedroom door, but not completely. As usual, there's a crack the light comes through. He gets undressed, sighs.

Kevin, in pyjamas in the hall, approaches on tiptoe.

Steve opens his closet. Takes out the large pouch. It's like it holds a secret. The *zzzzzzz* of the zipper; then, underneath, the red of the costume. Steve puts on the gold pants first. Pulls on the hems so they fall properly. Bare-chested in his winner's pants. Glances in the mirror. Behind the door, Kevin watches the metamorphosis. His father slowly becomes a superhero. Steve pulls the form-fitting jersey over his head. He looks strong, with his round shoulders and his broad back under the shiny fabric. Just one thing missing. *The* thing.

Kevin squirms, impatient, trips in the doorway. Holds his breath. Steve turns. Silence. Kevin, like a statue, stops moving.

Steve roots around in the large pouch and pulls out the last thing. He holds it at arm's length in front of him. It catches the light from the street, it catches the whole world; for an instant everything exists through the piece of red fabric that Steve, in a movement that's perfection, slips over his shoulders.

The transformation is complete. Big, head held high, with his cape on his straight back: he is the strongest man in the world.

Steve, his fingers blackened from his last day at the garage, clumsily tries to tie the cape. His fingers won't do what he wants. He gets impatient. Fuck. The thin tie breaks. Steve looks at himself in the mirror, squeezed into a cheap costume, a bit of string between his fingers. Closes his eyes, holds back tears.

Kevin tiptoes back to his bedroom. Heroes don't cry. He slams the door.

✦   ✦   ✦

Louise jumps. 'Goddamn paper-thin walls,' she mutters. She falls right back asleep on the sofa, with the stale remains of sex with end-of-day lovers: a porno film drools its light on her. In her room, Roxane is in pyjamas standing in front of the mirror. She delicately holds in her hands the picture of Anastasia, torn from the red book. Her eyes travel from the Russian face to her reflection. She explores all the contours: the roundness of the cheeks, the slight swell of the lip, the curl of the eyelashes. In front of the mirror, a long time, like that.

✦   ✦   ✦

Kevin in pyjamas, in front of the giant TV in the living room, is plugged into his machine and is shooting little men who run in vain to the four corners of the screen.

Steve roots around at the back of a drawer, irritated, his cape balled up on the counter.

Kevin looks at him out of the corner of his eye. Pauses the massacre. A little man is frozen, arms outstretched, exploding, the blood on pause, pooled in the middle of the screen. Kevin approaches his father.

'What are you looking for?'

Steve growls, his head in the drawer. Kevin takes the cape in his little hands. Steve snatches it back.

'Leave that alone. It's bad enough as it is.'

'What are you looking for, Dad?'

Steve dumps the contents of the drawer on the floor, kneels, searching.

✦   ✦   ✦

8:48. The time blinks on the microwave. Steve is kneeling in the middle of the kitchen. Kevin is standing behind him in the dark. The little man is still exploding in a frozen pool of blood, the still screen the only source of light. Kevin's little fingers, with absolute precision, slide a safety pin through the red cape. Kevin is focused.

— 44 —

'Lift your chin.'

Steve obeys without flinching.

'Okay, I'm going to use another one just to be sure.'

'Mmm.'

Steve keeps his chin up while Kevin, concentrating, slips a final pin through the red fabric.

'Okay, done.'

Steve stands up. The cape around his shoulders. Tugs on it. A jab to the right. A jab to the left. Leg lock, right jab, two rough power moves, and Kevin smiles.

'Is it holding?'

'It's holding.'

Steve puts on his long black coat over his costume and his winter boots. He opens the door.

'Dad, can I come?'

'No, Kev. Not too often, you know. It's expensive.' He pats him on the back. 'Finish your game and go to bed, okay?'

'Mmm.'

Steve barrels down the stairs.

'Bye, Dad!' Down the stairs: 'Kick his butt!'

The door to the apartment block slams. Kevin heads back into the apartment and goes back to his game. The half-blown-up little man is still frozen in his patch of blood. He looks at him for a moment. It's all over for him. Kevin, solemn, presses the PAUSE button. The little man finishes exploding, and the blood disappears. Kevin turns off the television.

Goes into his bedroom, opens his album, the one with the leather cover. The one his mother gave him. Inside, faces of all the wrestlers, with their autographs beside them: SmartFox with his rabid-fox mask, MegaStar in his old electric-blue costume, BadJo that time he grabbed Speedy by surprise. And Big, with his shiny red cape, Kevin sitting on his shoulders. He had won again. Always wins.

Kevin falls asleep with the album beside him.

◆ ◆ ◆

From the bowels of the church to the corner of the sidewalk, people are doing their best to exist. 'Killkillkillkillkillkill!' Heavy metal music reverberates from the basement to the street. Under the blank screens of the pawnshop, Kelly and Kathy caress each other to the syncopated rhythm of the wrestlers. 'Killkillkillkillkillkill!' while in the ring, Big throws Fighter into the ropes, 'Killkillkillkill!' Under the blank screens, Kelly and Kathy make love.

✦ ✦ ✦

The sound of a key in the lock. Kevin opens his eyes a little. 00:12. Face pressed in his album. Steps in the hallway. His father's shadow for a moment in the crack of the door. Behind the shadow, his smell: a mix of sweat and warm beer. Then the sound of fabric that he carefully puts away in his closet, the weary *zzzzzzzzz* of the large pouch that contains the hero, until next time. A sigh.

Steve turns out the lights, and Kevin goes back to sleep.

четыре
4

The doorbell rings. Mélissa opens her eyes in her mother's bed, too big for her. It's 7:00 a.m. It's her! She leaps out of bed, throws herself at the door, opens it. It's the guy for the rent, looking surly.

'I'm here to collect.'

'Collect what?'

The big man looks around. His little rat eyes roam shamelessly from the living room to the kitchen.

'Collect what?'

'Where's your father?'

'He's not my father.'

'Then the guy who takes care of you. Where's he?'

'At work.'

'Ah.'

His rat eyes everywhere again. It's like they're boring through the walls.

'Bye.'

Mélissa shuts the door. Fuck. She looks around the apartment. Old dishes and empty cans, liquor bottles and chip bags, clothes and DVDs scattered on the floor. And the two boys sleeping fully dressed in the middle of the living room. Fuck, fuck. Mélissa shakes them.

'C'mon, guys! Get up. We have to clean up before school. Dammit, Francis. You pissed your pants!'

Mélissa collapses in the middle of the mess. This morning, she would like to disappear. Not forever. She would come back once she is an adult. Once she has grown up, hair untangled, with a job and a house. And a dog. Maybe a dog. The past, the present, whoever wants it can have it.

Roxane is in the living room. Her mother is still sleeping. Roxane is talking on the phone in a hushed voice.

'Hi, Dad.

'(…)'

'Did I wake you up?'

'(…)'

'It's 'cause I wanted to ask a question. Was Grandma Russian?'

'(…)'

'Where's St. Hippolyte?'

'(…)'

'Oh.'

'(…)'

'No, just wanted to know. My teacher said I look Russian.'

'(…)'

'Yeah, I know. I just wanted to find out. Go back to bed. Bye.'

✦ ✦ ✦

'Dad! Dad! Wake up!'

Kevin is in his underwear, bags under his eyes.

'Dad! You're going to be late for the garage!'

Steve's eyes fly open, he snaps up in bed, looks at the time.

'You're going to be late for work, Dad, c'mon!'

Kevin climbs on the bed and jumps up and down, a foot on either side of his father. Steve groans and flops back down.

Kevin stops jumping. ' … Dad?'

'Mmm … no work today.'

'Oh.'

Kevin looks down at his father for another minute. His stubble, the dark circles, the drool from the night drying on his cheek. Kevin gently climbs off the bed and leaves, closing the door behind him.

✦ ✦ ✦

'It's World War Eight, there are 233 clans, and you have to choose yours, your allies, your spies, your vessel. When you start, you have ten more lives, so you don't die right away. Wanna play?'

Steve is eating toast, reading the *Journal de Montréal*. 'No.'

Kevin keeps playing alone.

On a full page, a girl is split open; she's bathing in her own blood. Her eyes are open. Steve lingers on her eyes. He would like to know what colour they are, but the newspaper is black and white. They could have made an exception for her. Show her eyes in colour, at least for today, I dunno.

'Why'd they do that?'

Out of the corner of his eye, Kevin continues to invade new virtual countries. 'What?'

'The girl.'

He asks the question every time. Can't get used to it.

Steve lights a smoke.

'To remind you that you're lucky, or to warn you not to do anything stupid, or to remind you that people are shit. Take your pick.'

A knock at the door. Kevin hits PAUSE, jumps up, and goes to answer it. It's the rent guy.

'It's the rent guy!'

'Mr. Gingras,' the rent guy grumbles.

Steve gets up from the table and does up his bathrobe. 'Hi. I can't pay you right now. I don't have the money.'

'Oh. So when?'

'Soon, I'll get it.'

'So I'll come back in three days?'

'Yeah. Three days.'

Steve closes the door.

He goes to sit down, stubs out his cigarette. Kevin watches him.

'How come you don't have any money, Dad?'

Steve lights another cigarette.

'Eh, Dad?'

' … I don't have money because I don't have a job.'

' … '

'The garage didn't need me anymore.'

Kevin starts the game again.

Between puffs, Steve starts skating a little. 'It's too bad you weren't at the last match. I had a couple of pretty slick holds.'

Shoot, shoot, shoot. Kevin isn't listening.

Steve goes back to his paper, but he can't see anything anymore.

◆ ◆ ◆

'Francis! Dammit. Put this back. I just put it away!'

Mélissa picks up everything off the floor and puts it on the sofa. At least it's not on the floor anymore.

All the dishes in the sink, all the clothes in the washer, all the leftovers in the fridge, it's all rotten, it stinks, everything stinks, Mélissa dumps everything on the floor – the food, the pots, her little brothers – she dumps them on the floor and kicks them.

◆ ◆ ◆

Mélissa is washing the kitchen floor. On the radio, Madonna is singing 'Like a Virgin.' The boys are at school but she isn't going. She's decided. At least there are some advantages to being on your own.

The phone rings. Mélissa turns down the radio and answers.

'Hello?'

A serious voice on the line, a voice that enunciates every syllable, a voice from a world that looks down on hers. Mélissa holds her head up and puts some gravitas into her little girl's voice.

'This is Mélissa.'

'(…)'

'Hello.'

'(…)'

'Not here.'

'(…)'

'Working.' Mélissa makes her voice curt. 'Yes, everything's fine.'

'(…)'

'No, there's nothing, ma'am.'

The voice on the other end insists.

'Okay, I'll take it down anyway.'

'(…)'

'Okay, thanks then.'

Mélissa hangs up. She throws out the paper where she has just written down the number of the bitch from Youth Protection. She should have said: 'Hello? Bitch from Youth Protection? Oh, yes, my mother's told me so much about you. No, no, nothing good, no.' She better not show up here.

Mélissa turns up the sound, pours diluted bleach on the floor, and mops while dancing to 'Like a Virgin.'

✦ ✦ ✦

Steve, in the kitchen, hunched over the *Journal*. He is deciphering the classified ads. His thick finger runs over the small letters. Small letters that make or break a life.

He opens a beer, downs it, opens another.

His thick finger has no more traces of sludge, not even under the nail, not even in the folds of the skin. His thick finger with no personality continues its path in vain over the small letters that ask for everything he isn't. Not meant to exist.

Downs his beer, opens another.

✦ ✦ ✦

Kevin goes down to class. Holds the handrail because today he's afraid of falling.

The teacher says the names of the animals in the nativity scene, in English. *The ox and the donkey watch the baby.*

Kevin lays his head on his desk, his cheek plastered against his Batman book. Beside him, the crazy girl is talking to herself, meaningless words. He wants to tell her to shut up. He lifts his head, looks at her: 'Shut up,' he tells her. Puts his head back down on the desk.

Roxane couldn't give a shit; she can't hear anything anymore. *Snieg snieg snieg.* Her eye wanders to the light from outside while the teacher places the figurines from the nativity scene under a fake Christmas tree that doesn't smell like anything.

Other girls ended up making Mary. She's beige, she has no smell, no boobs. Flat as a board, Mary. Eat shit, Mary.

The donkey is grey, the ox is brown, and it's almost Christmas. Things are going really well in the remedial class.

✦   ✦   ✦

Kathy and Kelly are clinging to each other under their soaked covers. Meg is crouched beside them. Kathy holds the joint out to her. On the TVs, time has stopped on the bands of colour that bleed onto the grey of Rue Ontario. Kathy inhales the smoke.

'So apparently women think more about shopping than making love.'

Kelly bursts out laughing.

'It's true. They said so on TV. Three out of four women think about buying something, a dress or whatever, every sixty seconds. I mean, come on! I counted, that's 960 times a day, for fuck's sake.'

Kathy accepts the joint back from Meg. Takes a long drag.

Silence.

Meg, her voice trembling from the cold: 'Well, I'd like to shop instead of making love.'

'You don't make love. Here, take some covers.'

Kelly holds out the sleeping bag, and Meg drapes it over her shoulders.

'It's true. You don't make love. That's not making love.'

'So what am I doing then?'

'Well, you fuck.'

Silence. Between confusion and reflection.

' ... I make love to them.'

'They buy you, you sell yourself, you–'

'I make love to them. I know what I do, for fuck's sake. I'm the one doing it!'

'Okay, okay. Here, have a puff.'

Meg has a puff. 'It's true, or else what? If I don't make love and I don't shop, then what the hell am I doing?'

'Don't cry, Meg.'

'Yeah, don't cry, Meg.'

◆ ◆ ◆

Roxane and Louise are in the living room, in front of the TV. Under the spotlights, they're deciding who to eliminate. Roxane on one sofa, Louise on another.

'Pass the tobacco.'

'He's going to get booted off.'

'Yeah, for sure.'

They roll cigarettes together. Roxane concentrates because she's going to bring some to her father. The nicest ones, the best-rolled ones.

Outside, the yellow brigade has its equipment out: snowplows, scrapers, spreaders, loaders. All the machines are out. It's been snowing all day, and it's still coming down. The sidewalks are going to be a big job.

Footsteps on the stairs. It's the stepdad coming home. A case in his hands.

Roxane looks up. At him. And her mother. Puts the half-rolled cigarette on the table. Gets up. Her mother heads her off.

'Oh, c'mon, Roxane, relax!'

'No, I have stuff to do. Homework.'

'Hey! Enough of this crap! Sit down! I'm not drinking! Jesus, quit running off every time you see a bottle. You're the one who's sick!'

Roxane sits back down.

'The edge of your ass on the edge of the sofa. You comfortable?'

Roxane backs up a little, body stiff.

'She's scared of me! She's scared of me, for chrissake!'

Roxane's mother opens a beer. *Phsst.* The sound. Just the sound ties her stomach in a knot.

'I'll be back, Mom, I – '

'Go on, run away. Go back to your little world. It's so much nicer there than here, isn't it?'

Louise takes a swig. She wishes Roxane would stay there with her, rolling cigarettes, watching TV. She takes another swig.

◆　◆　◆

Rue Aylwin. Night falling.

Kevin drags his feet through the snow. It leaves tracks, like he has super-big feet. Imagine being kicked by feet that big. Kevin walks backward, looking at his giant footprints all the way home.

His key is hanging around his neck; he looks for it under the umpteen layers of his snowsuit, finds it. Opens the door – it's dark inside – turns on the TV.

Steve is there, sitting in the dark, beer in hand.

'Dad?'

Steve takes a swig.

Kevin doesn't take his eyes off him while he takes off his snowsuit. His father looks unhappy. That much he knows. What to do about it he doesn't know. Kevin sits on the floor, at his father's feet. Slips a game into the PlayStation – PLAY – and hands Steve a controller.

'C'mon, one game with me.'

A moment goes by while Kevin hopes. Steve puts down the beer and grabs the controller. Kevin suppresses a wide grin and grabs the other one.

◆　◆　◆

Sitting on her bed, Roxane tears photos from the red book. In addition to the paper tearing, she hears the regular sound of gunfire coming from the wrestler's apartment next door. But it's in her own living room that war preparations are underway.

She sticks images to her bedroom walls. A map of Russia and, beside it, the Kremlin in winter. She also has a picture of a skating rink in the middle of Moscow with crowds of tiny people. There's probably music playing, you can see it, practically hear it. It's obvious. There is music in this picture. Roxane glues Anastasia beside her bed.

She flips through what's left of the book. A few pictures left. A river, wide, calm, gentle. It's pretty. That's where she would go with her boat.

Roxane cuts, concentrates, glues.

The Volga runs through her bedroom, its whitewater foam masking the shouting that gradually takes over from the living room. Roxane holds her breath and dives, body and soul, into the Volga.

✦ ✦ ✦

'AHHHH! Jesus H. Christ, you're good!

'Yeah, but Dad, I play all the time! It's your first try! Oh, shit! You did that on purpose! You distracted me!'

The two of them are standing in the dark, bodies bent over the light of the screen. Kevin's shining eyes dart quickly at his dad. He's almost making him happy.

'Let's go, let's go.'

✦ ✦ ✦

Shostakovich, beginning of the record. Roxane puts on her headphones and lies down on the bed. She loses herself in Moscow, a big white city with its rows of snow-covered roofs. 'From the Es-pla-nade of the Krem-lin, the view of Mos-cow stret-ches before you. You are in a dif-fer-ent world …'

BANG! The door opens, the light hits Roxane, her mother is yelling, but Shostakovich is there, between them and her. He is protecting her. Her stepfather grabs her mother from behind by the hair. Roxane can make out screams underneath the sultry bow. Roxane, a hostage of the scene, takes in the absurd choreography.

Her mother, on the floor, face contorted, is having trouble getting up. He's got her by the neck. She bites, he hits, she screams.

Roxane is petrified.

The music.

Her mother's face.

The music.
Her mother getting up off the floor.
Him going to the kitchen.
Her, screaming, following him.
In the kitchen, knives.
Shostakovich can't protect her against knives.
Roxane runs.

In pyjamas in the storm, Roxane walks by the prostitutes.
Just one or two of them. The storm has hit everyone.

Roxane runs along the river. Snow in her eyes, a scream in her head.

On the shore of the Volga, Roxane waits for a boat that doesn't come.

Roxane is bundled in a wool blanket under the fluorescent lights of the police station. *Snieg, dymn, toumann, louna, zima, oblako* – like a story just for her that tells no tale, where there is nothing to understand, where nothing hurts – *snieg, dymm, toumann, louna, zima, oblako. Snieg, dymm, toumann, louna, zima, oblako.*

'It's okay.' Roxane is trembling. 'It's okay.' Roxane is rocking.

They picked her up in the street. It's not the first time. They're waiting for her to warm up, then they'll take her home.

+ + +

It's midnight. The two of them are bare-chested in the living room, sweating as if they had done battle for real. Kevin is eating a hot dog, looking outside.

'She ran away again.'

Downstairs, Roxane gets out of the police car, escorted by two men in uniform.

'Dad! The neighbour ran away again.'

'Mmm.'

Steve is eating his hot dog, head in the clouds, butt on the sofa.

Kevin stands in front of him. 'Dad?'

'Mmm?'

'I want you to teach me to wrestle.'

Steve laughs, but Kevin insists. 'Seriously, Dad. I'm serious.'

'Oh, come on, have you taken a look at yourself?'

'I WANT YOU TO TEACH ME!'

+ + +

Louise at the door, a bit drunk, exchanges a few words with the officers.

The smell of chaos lingers in the apartment, but a ceasefire has been signed for the night.

Roxane goes to bed.

+ + +

'Ouch!'

Steve holds Kevin on the floor. Kevin strains to get up.

'Now, you fake. You move your head over like this, and – *bang!* – you get up.'

The two of them are standing in the kitchen.

'And then – *schlack!* – into the ropes, hard, with everything you've got!'

Kevin throws his tensed little body at his father. Steve plays along and, as if he were blown backward, hurtles to the other end of the room and falls to the floor.

'Ah! I'm out!'

Kevin lifts his arms in the air.

'AND THE WINNER IS!'

Roxane's bedroom.

Looks at the clock. Fuck. She didn't wake her up. Again.

It's dark outside. It's dark inside.

Roxane gets up, blanket over her shoulders. Opens the door. Drags her feet to the cold living room.

Beer bottles all over the place; her mother too.

Roxane approaches her, hand over her mouth, close. Waits a moment. She's alive.

Pulls the sheet over her and goes back to bed.

+ + +

The hems of the skirts tickle her face. Mélissa is sitting in the closet surrounded by fabric. Takes a deep breath.

Smells leave too.

Mélissa slips her feet into the black shoes. Women's shoes. Meg wore them on big nights. Her birthday, Christmas. Or sometimes she liked putting them on to have a coffee at Sandy's, or just to do groceries. That meant she was in a good mood and that you should go with her because it would be fun. When Meg put her black shoes on, it meant they would stop at the park and run after pigeons and hurl insults at them, they would share a pudding chômeur with one spoon at Clo's and drink coffee even though she's not old enough, they would laugh at people and the crazy lives they invented for them, then they would race to the grocery store. Mélissa would be faster than her mother because with the black shoes you run pretty, not fast. At the grocery store, Meg would hang off the back of the cart, and Mélissa would run and push. She would want to go fast so her mother would laugh louder, so Mélissa would get winded on the way to the frozen-food aisle, where they would concentrate for a minute to find pizza pockets and pogos for the boys, then they would start rolling again. If her mother were in a really good mood, they would buy a box of Fudgsicles, and the four of them would eat them in silence on the balcony, fast so they didn't melt all over the place. But they would melt anyway.

Mélissa emerges from the closet, the shoes on her feet. Just a while longer and they'll fit perfectly. Looks in the mirror. Takes a few steps. Crosses the bedroom once, then again, sashaying. 'Hello, yes, a pudding chômeur a spoon a coffee please!' Meg reborn on her lips for a moment, Meg, light and feminine. Meg laughing and wearing black shoes.

'MEEEEL!'

The boys' voices in the kitchen.

'MEEEEL! I'm hungry!'

Mélissa emerges, shoes on her feet. She makes porridge for the boys. Each clack of a shoe between the fridge and the stove, between the stove and the table, each clack is like a balm to her heart.

◆ ◆ ◆

The schoolyard.

Leaning against a wall, eyes staring off into space, Roxane talks, half mumbling, in an invented language.

Children hurl words and pebbles at her.

'She says she's Russian.'

'So why aren't you there?'

'Because I moved here?'

'You're mental.'

'No.'

'Yes, you're mental.'

'Go back to where you came from, you fucking headcase!'

'Okay.'

◆ ◆ ◆

Mélissa is in running shoes and wears a scarf tied carefully around her neck.

She walks along the prostitutes' street. Slows down once she's across the street from them. Catches her mother's eye.

The cars go by between them, as if to remind them of the space that separates them. The fifty metres that tears them apart. When a car passes, Mélissa squints and focuses her eyes to catch all the little bits of her mother that can still be caught. Through the windows, over the shoulder of the driver, a shoulder – a hip. Behind the rolling wheels, blurry, a shin – an ankle.

When there's a break in the cars, she looks at all of her mother.

Today she has something for her.

She places an envelope in the gap between the gutter and a tire at rest.

◆   ◆   ◆

Meg waits for her daughter to move on. Her eyes glued to the white of the paper against the grey of the street, she crosses. She holds the envelope in her hand. A piece of her daughter. She holds the envelope awhile longer before opening it. Then, with her fingertips, she opens it. She hangs on through her pink nails. She is trembling.

Cursive letters. Pretty. She has good penmanship.

'Your boyfriend left. We're all alone at home.'

She holds the letter in her hand. He left. They're alone. Fuck.

Fuck fuck fuck.

They're going to get picked up, for sure. They're going to get placed in some shitty conditions far away, fuck FUCK!

◆   ◆   ◆

The white library under the school's fluorescent lights. In the middle, the 'World' aisle.

Roxane searches. Her long fingers brush the spines of the books. *Frrrrrrrrrrrr.*

Alone in the middle of the World, Roxane is searching for herself. Alone in the middle of the aisle, Roxane collapses.

✦ ✦ ✦

Ms. Bilodeau is bent over her. She stopped reading just as James was leaning toward Mia's lips, on page 42, when Roxane collapsed in the middle of the aisle with a dull thud. Her face is hovering over Roxane, eyes worried. Hands under her head, she gently lifts her. Roxane feels good, like this, lying in her aisle with Ms. Bilodeau.

'Are you okay, Roxane?'

'Yes.'

'How do you feel?'

'Better.'

'What happened?'

'I was dizzy.'

'You fainted?'

'It's seasickness.'

'To be seasick, you have to be on water, Roxane.'

'No.'

'No?'

'I have all the water in the world inside me. Didn't you know?'

In the middle of the enormous library, between a thousand warehoused stories, two castaways. A fleeting moment in the aisle of the World.

✦ ✦ ✦

Steve is walking along Ontario, facing into the cold.

It's a cold that gets inside you as if you were its home. There's nothing you can do about it – you can be wearing fifteen layers and it blasts right through them.

Steve goes into a french-fry joint. Heads to the counter.

'Coffee, please.'

The waitress serves him a black coffee in a Styrofoam cup.

'Thanks.'

He adds sugar.

To the waitress: 'Don't suppose you're looking for someone for deliveries?'

She shakes her head.

Steve drinks his coffee, pays, and leaves.

◆　◆　◆

Incredulous, Roxane holds a violin in her hands as if it were a red-hot ember.

'Happy?'

'Yes.'

'My son doesn't play anymore. He never really played. I wanted him to … Anyway. You like the violin, right?'

'…'

'We'll need to find you lessons now. You can touch it. It's yours.'

Roxane brings the violin to her stomach.

Hugs it against her like a life preserver.

'Thank you.'

◆　◆　◆

Five o'clock. The kid's late.

At that moment, footsteps on the stairs. Louise smiles. Tells herself she's a crap mother, but she's a mother all the same. They can't take that away from her.

She's had only two beers. Maybe three.

'Hi, sweetie.'

'Hi, Mom.'

Roxane hugs the black case against her stomach.

'What's that?'

'A violin.'

'A violin?'

'The librarian gave it to me.'

'What for?'

'To play.'

'Let's see.'

A pause. Takes a breath. Approaches. Kneels down. Puts the case down, gently.

Louise, understanding the tenuousness of the moment, kneels too, awkwardly.

Mother and daughter face each other, between them the black case Roxane gently opens.

The violin appears. Like a sunbeam scratching the grey of the room, a scar of the ugliness of their life; mother and daughter look at the perfect object.

Too nice for them. Too clean, too shiny, too smooth.

'You're going to play it?'

Roxane looks at her mother from deep inside. Looks at her mother, her reflection in her eyes.

Roxane is looking at herself.

'You're going to play it?'

'Yes.'

✦ ✦ ✦

Mélissa is sitting facing the teacher who is trying in vain to catch her eye.

Mélissa has her feet crossed under the table. She furtively glances at her black shoes, which dangle nonchalantly.

'And how are things at home, Mélissa?'

'Good.'

'Good?'

'Yeah.'

'Look me in the eye, Mélissa.'

' … '

'You're wearing makeup?'

Silence.

'Yes.'

✦ ✦ ✦

Steve is still walking along Ontario. Crosses through a huddle of prostitutes. They're all there already. Must be close to five. Prostitutes keep time in the east end of the city, he thinks to himself. Eastern time. Not always at the same time, but always the right time. It makes him smile.

They would warm him up a little, but it would hurt even more to go back to the cold afterward. He is all too familiar with it. A woman's body makes him founder.

He walks by the garage.

Tony's there. He's reading the paper while he waits for cars. One comes in. It's Michel and his old powder-blue Mustang. It's breathtaking, all the same. It has a particular smell, of its time, something reassuring that smells like its era, that smells like the good ol' days.

Tony would call him to fill it up when it came in, because he knew the smell did something to him. Steve leaves before Tony spots him.

He walks briskly home.

It's empty and cold there too.

He cracks open a beer.

+ + +

Kevin stomps up the stairs, the music from his game in his gut, an action tempo full of suspense: someone is chasing him, he sneaks landing to landing, back pressed to the wall, looks left, right, takes the stairs four at a time, slams right into the big guy who collects the rent.

'Sorry!'

The big guy who collects the rent is coming out of Mélissa's. He's doing up a button on his shirt, putting his coat back on.

Through the doorway, Kevin sees Mélissa dressed in lace, like those bus shelter ads. She avoids his eyes: looks down at the ground and Kevin's eyes follow.

'Nice shoes!' he says.

Mélissa closes the door.

Kevin stands facing the big guy who collects the rent.

'Your dad home?'

'No. He's working. Is your dad home?'

Kevin flings himself at the next door, slides in his key, and in a flash he's inside.

Sigh of relief. He got away from the bad guy.

+ + +

'Hey, Dad!'

Kevin jumps on his father, uses his big night voice.

'He jumps on him, ladies and gentlemen, yes, he's going to drop him … '

'Stop it.'

Kevin keeps it up, going wild. 'And WonderKev grabs Big by the throat and – '

'I SAID STOP, GODDAMMIT!'

Kevin stops, surprised.

Sniffles. Chews on his lip.

Goes to the fridge. Pours a glass of Coke.

Comes back to sit in the living room, turns on the TV.

'Turn that off.'

Kevin turns to look at Steve.

'I said turn that off.'

'Why?'

'Come on. Don't you have homework to do? Something to make you smart, school stuff? Do it.'

'I'm going to do it after, I … '

Steve turns off the TV. 'You'll do it now. How are you going to get smart otherwise? What are you going to do with your life, huh? Sit on your ass watching goddamn stupid cartoon men tear around all over the place? Practise shooting fake people, with a fake gun in a fake fucking apocalypse? Huh? Not too smart, that. Go on, get out of here!'

Kevin's lips are bleeding.

Doesn't move.

'MOVE IT!'

+ + +

It's late.

Silence in the apartment.

The blood has dried on Kevin's lips. He is drawing, absorbed.

Doesn't hear Steve approach.

Over his shoulder.

'That school work?'

Kevin jumps, turns toward him. Steve, awkward, clears his throat.

Kevin looks at him. Thinks he looks rough. Tired. His eyes are drooping. For the first time he thinks he looks old.

'Don't look at me like that!'

Kevin goes back to his drawing.

Steve stays standing behind him. Tries to find the words. ' … When was that?'

Kevin keeps his nose in his drawing. 'The semifinal. When MadMax clotheslined you in the right corner.'

'But I came back after that!'

' … I know.'

'You're not drawing that, are you?'

'No.'

Silence.

'Time for bed, little man.'

'Mmm.'

Silence.

'If you want, on Friday, you can come to the match.'

Kevin lifts his head, but doesn't look at his father. 'Okay.'

Steve closes the door.

Early morning. Mélissa leaves before she used to, because sometimes when it's early there are still prostitutes on the corner. Maybe she'll still be there. The boys follow her in silence; they're still half-asleep in their puffy jackets, dragging their feet, leaving snail-like trails on the ground.

She's there, on the other side of the court-ordered fifty metres. But she isn't looking at her. Mélissa slows down a little. She just wants her to look at her for a heartbeat, just a bit, just, you know, for her to look at her …

No. She has her back turned. As if she hasn't seen her. If Roxane could cross the street, she would spit in her face or bite her neck because her neck smells good, so good.

Stupid fifty metres.

Mélissa swallows. Lifts her head, starts walking, says, 'C'mon, guys!'

As she is walking away, her eyes catch the white against the grey. Her letter. She didn't even pick it up.

She bends over, picks it up, opens it.

Finds twenty bucks and a note: 'Act like I'm there. Nothing different. Take care of the boys, and if anyone calls, say he found a job and he's not there right now and everything is fine. Don't tell them you're alone.'

It's the first letter she's ever received from her mother.

She reads it again.

'Act like I'm there. Nothing different. Take care of the boys, and if anyone calls, say he found a job and he's not there right now and everything is fine. Don't tell them you're alone.'

I'm not alone.

Okay. Okay, Mom.

On the other side of the street, Meg has turned around. A big truck passes.

Then Meg's not there anymore.

'Let's go, guys, c'mon!'

The snails advance, yawning.

Mélissa, her hand deep in her pocket, the letter deep in her hand, goes to school.

◆ ◆ ◆

Steve has put on a belt to hold up his pants and shined his shoes. It made his fingers dirty, and for a second (no more), he got emotional (just a little).

Now he is standing in front of a big, thick-set guy who looks off to the side while Steve talks.

Steve is nervous but tries not to show it.

'Well, I've got experience with cars; I worked at a garage for a long time. I'm a good mechanic, I – '

'You see any connection between cars and snow blowers?'

'Well, you drive 'em, I mean, it's … I like storms, I … can kick up a pretty good one myself.'

The joke falls flat. The guy doesn't even spot it.

'Our guys have experience with big cleanup jobs. Handling a vehicle like that isn't like handling a car … You'd have to start at the bottom of the ladder.'

'Okay, what's the bottom of the ladder?'

'Well, we don't have anything right now.'

◆ ◆ ◆

Roxane leaves the library. Runs into Mélissa in the hallway.

They look at each other and know they would be less alone together, but neither of them knows what a bond looks like.

'Hi!'

'Hi!'

So they just cross paths.

✦ ✦ ✦

They got her violin lessons at school. They're supposed to be just for the normals. But they made an exception. For her. The teacher's name is Caroll. He knows Shostakovich and was surprised Roxane knew him too.

She practises at lunchtime to catch up to the others. She practises on the same floor as the library. The floor with the normal classes. She is normal from noon to one, every day.

Has to practise a lot, because there's a concert coming up.

A real one. With an audience.

✦ ✦ ✦

A video poker bar. In the thick fog of last night's bender, the guys hide behind their steins, letting their lives dribble into them.

Steve stands tall in front of the bar, staring at a Latino guy squeezed into his tight T-shirt, would like him to tell him about his country some night, at the end of the bar, if he has any memory of it.

'You know how to mop?'

He's lost his accent. Or just forgot it.

'We need a guy on the floor ... '

'Yeah. Yeah, I can mop.'

'Nights.'

' ... I can't do nights, I – '

'That's what we need.'

'It's 'cause I have a kid. I'm on my own with him. I can't leave him alone at night, he – '

'That's what we need.'

Steve leaves.

He sees the huddle of prostitutes in the street. It's six o'clock. He needs some affection.

'Meg?'

His neighbour. All that's left of her are her eyes. Used to be pretty. They head off together.

◆ ◆ ◆

It's slushy. Mélissa's feet are wet, and her pants are soaking up the slop from the street.

Her mother isn't with the group of prostitutes. Mélissa looks at them one by one.

It's always the same ones, huddled together. Like a girl gang. There's one close to her age. She's skinny; in her high heels she's like a raggedy stork. She looks back at her. Mélissa spits on the ground. Doesn't like the girl. Little whore.

She slides a new envelope under the tire, then leaves, staring the girl down.

◆ ◆ ◆

It's dark on Rue Ontario. Meg is freezing.

Has a hard time opening the envelope, her hands are trembling so much. She asks the young girl to help her.

The stork grabs the envelope, tears it, takes out the note, reads it to Meg.

'I can't get the washing machine going.'

The stork looks at Meg.

'Gimme a cigarette.'

'Here.'

'Thanks.'

Meg can't hold the cigarette in her hands. The stork holds it so she can smoke. One puff at a time.

'Want me to answer for you?'

Meg nods.

◆ ◆ ◆

Steve pulls on his tights in front of the mirror.

Kevin is sitting on the edge of the bed, feet dangling. He looks at his father's reflection in the mirror.

Steve puts on his skin-tight T-shirt, adjusts the sleeves.

'Did your shirt shrink, Dad, or what?'

Steve looks at him, surprised.

Looks at himself again in the mirror.

'Huh … I don't know … Fuck.' Steve sucks in his gut.

'Put the cape on.'

'Huh?'

'Put the cape on overtop. Maybe it won't show so much.'

Steve takes the cape out of the closet. Slips it over his shoulders. Attaches it. 'So?'

Kevin gives his approval. 'That's better.'

Silence.

'Dad?'

'No, little man. Not enough money.'

'But you promised!'

'Hey. Next week.'

◆　◆　◆

From the window, Big looks tiny on the street in the falling snow; even with his cape, people could crush him. Kevin blows warm air on the window and writes *fuck you* in the condensation.

◆　◆　◆

In an alley, on a stoop, Meg dictates to the stork, who concentrates on writing.

'First you put the clothes in. Whites and colours separately.'

'Wait, slow down!'

' …'

' … co-lours sep-a-rate … Okay, then what?'

'You put the blue liquid in the little holder, the one on the right.'

'… in the lit-tle hol-der …'

'On the right.'

'On the right.'

'Shut the door tight so the …'

'Shut the … You okay, Meg?'

In an alley, the day is ending. What's left of two women do laundry.

◆ ◆ ◆

The room in the church basement is full. It's a big night. Big is taking on a young new wrestler, FastAss, with a rounded ass and the face of a champ. Two mothers in sweatsuits are sharing a cigarette and jiggling their strollers. Two teenagers are selling hot dogs and soft drinks between French kisses that are heating up the air. Pot-bellied old friends touch cups with the soft click of plastic, to Big's health. Backstage, he ties his laces. The master of ceremonies comes over.

'New game plan, Big …'

◆ ◆ ◆

Run. Run. Run. Kevin crosses Rue Hochelaga, zips between two cars, splits the huddle of prostitutes in two, stumbles, gets back up, run, run run.

◆ ◆ ◆

The master of ceremonies in a black tank top announces the match.

'YO-YO-YO-YO!'

Around the ring, applause, whistles, and shouts.

'HOW'S EVERYONE DOING TONIGHT?'

The shouts get a little louder. The music keeps pace.

'OKAY, LET'S GET RIGHT TO IT, 'CAUSE THAT'S HOW WE ROLL, LADIES AND GENTLEMEN, LET'S GIVE A BIG HAND FOR OUR MAGIC CHAMPION … THE INCREDIBLE BIIIIG!'

From behind a cloud of smoke, under blood-red lights, ushered in by heavy metal music, Big appears. He walks confidently, grasps some hands around the ring before climbing into it. Takes a lap to cheers, cape fluttering in the wind.

'YEAH! AND TONIGHT, CHALLENGING OUR NATIONAL TREASURE, BIG, LADIES AND GENTLEMEN, PLEASE WELCOME A NEWCOMER, FASTASS!'

The bells chime from the top of the church: the match is starting.

The basement door opens a crack. Kevin slips through it. All eyes are on the ring. The fat cashier is looking the other way. The spotlight is on the master of ceremonies. Kevin slips in without paying.

Sweating. Happy. He hasn't missed anything.

The match can start.

DING DING DING

The music fades out; all eyes in the crowd are glued to the ring.

'LET'S GO, BIG! TAKE THE KID OUT!'

✦ ✦ ✦

Meg jabs the syringe into the crook of her arm. A beat. Her face toward the sky.

A sigh that travels across the street.

Mélissa, pressed against a wall, would like to melt into it, become a red brick.

From the other side of the street, her mother's shadow and an impaled arm.

The arm she would like to have all to herself. That she waits patiently for, always.

This arm broken shrivelled jabbed emptied.

Mélissa vomits on her black shoes.

✦ ✦ ✦

In the ring, Big and FastAss signal their hate with trash talk and fake blood.

The crowd is going wild.

'BIG, BIG, BIG! HAMMER HIM! HAMMER HIM! HARDER!

They are shouting; they are shouting their week away, shouting their heads off; they are fighting without fighting, from their guts, with all of their pent-up rage – you find your winners where you can or you're through.

It's a party, so order another hot dog, Big's going to play hard tonight.

✦ ✦ ✦

Meg crumples to the sidewalk. A dull thud, no cry, nothing.

She crumples in silence, which makes it worse.

Mélissa would have crossed the street would have lifted her mother would have got her to her feet would have looked her in the eye would have asked her if she's okay.

On the other side of the street, Mélissa turns her back and goes home to clean her black shoes.

✦ ✦ ✦

Big misses a hold, takes a hit right in the face.

Kevin staggers, takes the hit with him.

The crowd reacts with shouts of *holy shit*, and Big ends up pinned to the mat.

'C'MON, BIG! GET UP! KICK HIS HEAD IN!

Big gets up. Straightens his cape on his shoulders. Lifts his head to the kid. Hurls himself at him, yelling.

FastAss moves fast, dekes, turns, smashes him hard in the face with his fist, which the crowd takes in the gut, a *fffff*, like a wave on lips wet with warm beer travels through the room.

Big is holding his jaw.

Safe in his corner of the ring, the master of ceremonies is thrilled. The show is a hit. That's how he likes it.

'LADIES AND GENTLEMEN, BIG IS WORN OUT!'

Kevin is hot. Wipes his forehead, his lips are wet – shit, it's blood – looks at the ring, come on, come on, LET'S GO, BIG! KILL HIM, DAMMIT! YOU CAN DO IT!

Big gets back up, like a projectile. Jumps on FastAss and grabs his head, pulls his hair, pins him against the ropes, rage in his belly, growls, fights, doesn't want to die – FastAss screams.

The master of ceremonies blows the whistle.

'LOW BLOW, BIG! LOW BLOW!'

FastAss holds his head, turns to the crowd, points to Big in his corner of the ring.

FastAss is enjoying himself, Big isn't.

❖ ❖ ❖

Mélissa enters the apartment. It's havoc rather than a home.

She runs warm water over her black shoes.

The boys are asleep in the bedroom. Mélissa goes over to their bed. They are sleeping huddled against each other. Their faces are peaceful and their fists are balled.

They may be dreaming. Or not.

Mélissa spits on them. Once, twice.

❖ ❖ ❖

A few boos can be heard in the room.

The opponents are sent to their corners. Silence.

Kevin is sweating heat and blood. He's shaking in his shoes. Let's go. Let's go. Let's go. Don't do this to me. You can do it.

The words run in a loop in his head.

The master of ceremonies blows the whistle, and the match resumes. Big charges full throttle at FastAss, who catches him with a hook, sends him flying into the ropes, the crowd reacts, Big pulls himself together, jumps on FastAss.

The crowd is going crazy, and from between the ropes, the master of ceremonies' eye gleams.

Big grabs a chair and with everything he's got hits FastAss once, twice, three times, in the face, on the back, in the ribs, take that! and that! and that! The crowd goes wild. FastAss sidesteps, grabs the chair from Big's hands, throws it into the crowd, leaps on Big, hurls him to the ground, and jumps on him feet together, jumps jumps jumps …

The crowd counts: ONE, TWO, THREE.

Kevin, his mouth bleeding, shouts with everything he's got left LET'S GOOOOO, BIG! GET UP!

Big lifts his head. Manages to get up. FastAss jumps on him, grabs him by the neck, pins him.

Kevin freezes. Something like the end of the world.

◆ ◆ ◆

The shoes are soaking in the kitchen sink. Mélissa has emptied the contents of the cupboards onto the floor.

She searches through the bottoms of empty bags. Comes up empty.

Opens the fridge. Takes out the jar of mayonnaise.

Sits at the table and finishes the jar of mayonnaise with a little spoon.

Mélissa doesn't cry.

◆ ◆ ◆

Red night on Ontario, Kathy is being chewed out by an enraged gang member.

He holds her by the hair, her head thrown back, face tensed, she screams, Kelly jumps on him, bites him, but he's so much stronger, shoves her off, she crashes to the ground, the dogs are barking in every direction, the guy makes a fist and punches, hits Kathy's stomach, once twice three times, Kelly screams, then goes quiet, absorbs every blow; Kelly is crying, frozen as she watches. The guy shoves Kathy, who ends up sprawled on the ground, hands knotted at her stomach, which is on fire. Kelly jumps on her, wracked in sobs; she rubs her quickly all over, kisses her with haphazard little kisses, hurt, helpless.

People in the street just kept walking. Like the blows were a light rain, they walked faster.

Kelly holds Kathy in her arms. This is the only end of the world there is.

◆ ◆ ◆

FastAss is strutting like a peacock around Big, who is still, shoulders slumped, out of breath …

Behind the mic, the master of ceremonies shouts in an echo.

'KILL! KILL! KILL!'

The crowd shouts with him:

'KILL! KILL! KILL!'

Bam! Big takes a head-butt to the stomach, he is hurled into the ropes, then thrown to the ground. Kevin watches in silence.

A voice somewhere: 'LOSER!'

Kevin feels it. Like a shot from an M16 right in the gut. He spins around, searches for the source.

'LOSER!'

Again.

'LOSER!'

Stop.

'BIG, LOSER!'

Kevin reels.

The crowd rubs it in: 'LOSER! LOSER! LOSER!'

He plugs his ears.

Everywhere: 'BIG, LOSER! LOSER! LOSER!'

Kevin looks around him. It can't be. Big has never lost. Big is a winner. He can't lose now, like this. He can't.

'LOSER! LOSER! LOSER!'

Kevin gnaws on his lips again, is dizzy. This is how it happens? The end of the world?

'LOSER! LOSER! LOSER! LOSER! LOSER!'

It drops on Kevin like a nuclear bomb. Exhausted, he turns back toward the ring. His eyes burning, lips wet, forehead damp. Big lost.

He lost. Kevin looks at him. It was the only place he was still winning. He had no right to lose. No right.

His face covered with sweat and blood, Kevin shouts at the top of his lungs, louder than anyone else.

'LOSER! … LOSER! LOSER! LOSER!'

Big, pinned to the ropes, weak, turns toward Kevin. Looks at him. Right in the eye.

Kevin looks back at him and keeps shouting.

'LOSER! LOSER! LOSER!'

Tears on his enraged face.

'LOSER! LOSER! LOSER!'

FastAss delivers his final blow, fatal. Big crashes to the ground. He lost. The audience is going wild; the champ is lifted up in the air, his picture is taken, the loser is booed, and beneath the cries of the crowd and the music, *killkillkill*, under Kevin's glare, his cape is torn off and thrown to the ground.

Kevin in a fury drowning shoves the crowd snatches the cape from anonymous hands and rushes outside.

In the ring, the disgraced old champ calls out to him: 'Kevin!'

Kevin runs. As fast as he can. The red cape floats in the wind. On a wall behind him, graffiti yells, *The poor stay poor*. In his head, a hammer, *killkillkill* …

Mélissa, teetering on her shoes, goes down the stairs. Her face pale and her body in lace, she knocks on a door. The guy who collects the rent opens. Looks both ways before letting her in.

At the back of an alley for a break. In the city, a long body, insect-like, slowly curls up and lets out a hoarse cry. A crack in the night.
Meg.

Backstage, FastAss signs autographs and high-fives the fans. The master of ceremonies brings him a cold beer. More guys are getting ready around him.

Sitting on a stool in the corner, Big unties his shoes.

His makeup has run on his damp face.

'Steve, want a beer?'

Steve doesn't answer. His face is hard. Tensed.

FastAss opens his beer, downs it.

'Let him digest his defeat. A one-eighty like that can't be easy ... '

The master of ceremonies raises his beer to Steve. 'Cheers, man!'

Steve stays bent over his shoes, fingers tangled in the laces.

Silence backstage as the tough guys lower their voices out of respect for the defeated champ. Steve hates their whispering. He hates the smell of their sweat and their compassionate looks. Steve is ashamed. A tear falls on his shiny shoes. Steve gets up. Picks up his things. Leaves in silence.

✦ ✦ ✦

Steve walks into the apartment.

'Kev?'

He knocks on Kevin's door. No answer.

'Open the door, Kevin, come on ... '

No answer.

In the bedroom, the furious sound of guns. Nothing else. Steve is tired.

'Jesus, Kevin, Christ, it's just a game! That's the first time I've lost, come on! ... It's no big deal ... '

Gun gun gun.

'And I'm not going to take it lying down. You'll see at the next match.'

Silence.

Steve rubs his forehead, sighs. At the end of his rope. At the end of everything. He leans his head against the locked door.

'What were you doing there anyway? Eh!'

Gun gun gun.

'And I'll find another job soon … They said they might take me back at the garage … That would be pretty good, eh, Kev?'

Gun gun gun.

'Maybe you could even help me fill up the blue Mustang that smells like the old days!'

Gun gun gun.

'Eh, Kevin? …'

Gun gun gun.

Sigh.

'You'll see. Everything's going to be all right.'

Gun gun gun.

'It's going to be us two … We're going to stick together …'

Silence.

'It's going to be okay.'

Sigh.

'Kev, you listening? Eh?'

No answer.

Steve kicks the door, walks away.

In the bedroom the gunfire starts up again even louder.

Violin notes travel through the wall. It's pretty.

Mélissa, naked, is kneeling in front of the washing machine, her little piece of paper unfolded. She is following the instructions to the letter. She would wash the whole world's clothes, her little paper in front of her, her mother's voice in every gesture. She doesn't even need to try to smell the perfect scent of lost Sundays.

✦ ✦ ✦

The big room at the end of the hall. When Roxane walks to her violin class, she walks fast. Practically flies. There's always sun in the room.

Her seat: always in the middle of the others, up front. She doesn't need to hide or run away here, so she leaves the window seat to someone else. 'Hello, sir' to the teacher who is setting up the music stands in his spotless white shirt. 'Hello, Roxane.'

The other students come in slowly. The bows take flight, music comes to life, and Roxane along with it.

In this room, at this moment, she is like the other kids. And she wants everyone to know.

'That's good, Roxane. You're good.'

'What?'

'You're good.'

✦ ✦ ✦

Mélissa sits in front of the bathroom mirror. Makeup is spread out around her. She applies colour to her face, then her cheeks, lips, and eyes.

With a voice growing steadily less childlike, she talks to herself as she concentrates on her transformation.

'Hidden behind it … no one can see you anymore … Where is Mélissa?'

She stares at herself in the mirror.

'Not here.'

✦ ✦ ✦

With her long, skinny fingers her chipped red nails there is no woman left there's nothing there but bones wearing makeup. She opens a new letter left in the crack in the road, mailbox for scum.

'Come home, Mom.'

Sniffs.

Swallows.

Crumples the paper. Throws it in the gutter.

✦ ✦ ✦

'Mom, there's going to be a concert.'

'Huh?'

'At my school, there's going to be a concert.'

'Oh. You want to go?'

'Uh, no. I'm playing in it.'

'You're playing in it?'

'Yeah, me and a lot of other kids from school, you know, the normal classes.'

'I see.'

'There's going to be guests.'

'Who?'

'Well, parents.'

'Oh.'

Silence.

'You going to come?'

'I don't know.'

'Mom, you have to come. You're my guest.'
'I'll come. Yeah, I'll come.'

◆   ◆   ◆

Steve in the doorway, TV in his hands.
'I got no choice, Kev.'
Kevin stares at him.
Steve looks down at the floor. Leaves.
A gaping hole in the apartment: there's no screen left.
Kevin is frozen in the middle of the living room. Escape is no longer possible.

◆   ◆   ◆

Kelly in a hoarse voice on her piece of cardboard: 'Got any change, mister?'
Steve from behind his TV: 'What do you think I'm doing here?'
Steve heads into the pawnshop.

◆   ◆   ◆

A corner of the schoolyard. Screams. Two children ripping at each other's skin with their nails, sinking their teeth into one another, crying together and at each other, hating each other for everything that surrounds them.
Kevin fights, rage in his gut for all that he isn't.
A teacher cuts through the little jungle and grabs Mélissa by the collar as she keeps spitting in every direction. She's screaming she's going to kill someone, kill everyone, she is crying and choking. She goes down the hallway, held up by four solid arms.
On the ground, Kevin wipes the spit from his face with the back of his sleeve. His nose is bleeding.
Roxane goes over to him, holds out her hand. Kevin gets up on his own.
He wipes his bloody nose. Spits at Roxane's feet and takes off.

‹ ‹ ‹

The principal, looking annoyed, lips pinched, holds the phone and lets it ring.

'There's no answer.'

'He's at work, I'm telling you.'

Mélissa holds a facecloth with ice in it to her forehead.

Her feet are swinging, she wants to take off.

'Where does he work?'

'Deliveries.'

'Where?'

'Deliveries.'

'He does deliveries?'

'Yes.'

'Of what? Where?'

'I dunno.'

'You don't know. Okay, you're going to have to help me here, Mélissa, if you want this to turn out well for you.'

'Potatoes.'

'Sorry?'

'Delivers potatoes.'

'He works in a restaurant?'

'Yeah. But I dunno which one.'

Silence.

Mélissa gets up and takes off running.

‹ ‹ ‹

'Roooooooox! That's enough!'

The bow stops. Suspended in scrolls of smoke.

Silence.

In the living room, the television. A game show with people who are winning. Lucky.

The bow gently returns to the strings. Play quietly, so quietly.

A *ti*. The bow like a wave over the notes, a silent *ti* so as not to bother anyone, a *do* that answers quietly, a *so* that stealthily follows, the whole piece like that, suspended, notes in her head, above the winners, above the smoke, above the world, above the shit.

+ + +

Mélissa slows her pace.

On her way, she leaves a note in the crack in the gutter. The one from last night isn't there anymore. She looks across the road. Not one girl. They're all busy. It's cold outside, and guys want a little loving.

There are no prostitutes for little girls. Sucks.

8

D ay breaks on Rue Ontario.
   Kelly thinks it mightn't have bothered.

+ + +

Roxane is standing up tall in the entrance, her coat on.
   'Hey, you can't leave me all alone like this!'
   The ruins of a woman in a bathrobe, talking with eyes closed.
   'Mom, I have to go. I said I would go.'
   'Christ, I need you right now.'
   She can't dry out alone.
   'I'll be back later.'
   'No! Anyway, it's freezing outside. Stay here, Roxane … Please …
Mommy needs you …'
   Roxane goes down the stairs.
   'My whole body hurts!'
   Roxane leaves because her father is waiting for her. Her mother's
voice echoes in her stomach all day.

+ + +

He looks rough.
   Sitting at the end of the bed, his pants too short and his wool
sweater full of holes.
   He's too big for the bedroom. Looks like a kid being punished.
   The walls are yellow, the bed tiny, but it takes up the whole room.
There's a table where he's put his ashtray and piles the *Journal de*

Montréal, then three shelves with a box of cookies, pictures, and Roxane's drawings.

He'll be holed up here for a few more months. Giving himself a chance.

Not ready for the real world.

'It's dark at five o'clock. I go to bed once it's dark. It makes it go faster.'

Roxane is sitting at the end of the bed.

'Hey, take off your coat.'

She takes off her coat.

Marc looks down at the floor.

'You okay, Dad?'

Lifts his head. 'Yeah. Yeah, it's okay … There are good people here. This time it's for good … For good.'

' … '

'Do you still believe me?'

'Yes, I believe you.'

Silence.

'Your boat's getting dusty.'

'Huh?'

'Your boat. Getting dusty.'

◆　◆　◆

An episode of *Lost* is playing on the televisions. Kathy and Kelly like it. They've watched every episode. Even without the sound, they can follow it. A group is trying to survive. Doesn't get any simpler than that.

Some passersby stop to watch, head off again after a bit.

They must know how it ends. Who survives.

◆　◆　◆

One block away. Mélissa is sitting on the sidewalk. She's eating salted sunflower seeds, spitting the shells as far as she can to the street. On the other side, the huddle of prostitutes kills time waiting for clients.

Mélissa has put on her snow pants so she can hang out there as long as she needs to.

Six notes have piled up in the cracks in the gutter, and no one is picking them up.

Tough shit. She'll read them eventually, and it'll be more all at once. Like a little book.

Meg hasn't been there for a while. The stork occasionally glances at Mélissa.

Mélissa tries to spit her sunflower seed shell at her. Too far.

'Hey! Tell Meg there are notes here for her!'

The stork turns around. The other prostitutes too.

'Do you get it or are you deaf? Tell Meg to pick up her mail. It's important!'

The prostitutes stop talking and look at the little girl in her purple snowsuit.

Silence.

The stork walks toward the curb.

'Meg will be away for a bit.'

She has the voice of a child.

'Where is she?'

'She'll be back in a while. I'll tell her once she's back.'

'Where is she?'

'She's sick. She's resting.'

'Where?'

'…'

'WHERE?'

Mélissa grabs a handful of sunflower seeds, hurls them to the other side of the street. She's red, feels like throwing up.

'Here, eat that! Eat that!'

She throws her sunflower seeds, arm outstretched, another handful, and another, empties her bag.

The girls watch her in silence.

Mélissa is crying.

✦   ✦   ✦

'Look, Dad.'

Roxane takes her violin from its case.

She brings it to her shoulder. Slides the bow along the strings. A sustained, graceful gesture. A long, perfect note.

Marc, eyes glued to his daughter.

Love in his eyes, which hardly ever happens.

Another note. Longer, even more beautiful.

Marc's eyes move from the violin to his daughter, from his daughter to the violin.

Sticks his head out in the hall.

'Hey, come check this out, Jean-Luc! My daughter can play the violin!'

Roxane focuses. Another long note like a stream, perfect, delicate but solid, to the point that you could walk on it on tiptoe without falling.

Slowly, the guys file into the little bedroom.

A herd of men, flayed, the shards of a life, basement warriors, they all let the light in for a moment.

Mélissa walks slowly. She's broken a wing and is going home.

Roxane, clutching her violin, crosses the street.

In his bedroom, Marc lights a cigarette and watches her disappear into the night. Hopes life will take care of her. Leaning against the window is the gift she gave him a while ago. His little boat. With some of its sails still white. Marc takes the sailboat in his big hands, blows on it. The dust takes to the air.

He gently puts the boat back in front of the window. Outside, the storm blusters. Marc turns the boat so its nose is facing outside. Course set for the storm. A beat.

Marc turns out the lights and lies down.

✦ ✦ ✦

Roxane pushes open the door of the apartment block, goes inside. In the distance, she spots Mélissa advancing along the sidewalk. She looks small in the dark. As if she could disappear without anyone noticing.

Roxane waits for her, holds the door.

'Hi.'

' … '

Mélissa's hair is covered in snow.

She notices Roxane's case. 'You're the one playing the violin?'

Roxane nods.

They climb the stairs. Mélissa holds the handrail.

'Did you hurt yourself?'

'No.'

They get to their floor.

Roxane looks at Mélissa, who is trying to get her key in the lock. She can't do it. She's trembling.

'I'm playing a concert with guests soon. You can come if you want.'

Mélissa gets her key in the lock.

She pushes open the door. Looks at Roxane.

It's like even her eyes are cold.

She goes in.

Roxane stays there for a moment. Then she goes inside too.

It's sunny out. A true winter morning when people are scurrying and looking up to catch a few rays. Mélissa walks to school, the boys hanging off her coat.

The prostitute corner is empty. Meg must be sleeping. Mélissa thinks about her mother, who is sleeping.

The notes aren't in the cracks in the gutter anymore.

Yessss!

◆ ◆ ◆

For once everyone is looking at them. Kathy and Kelly. For a moment they exist. Finally, a light is shining on their life on the street, the time it takes to scream. Kathy's arms are being held behind her by a cop, who is putting handcuffs on while another one restrains Kelly, who is seething with rage, consumed – 'LET HER GO' – Kathy is pushed against the car – they're saying she killed someone – Kelly, released, rushes at the windows, 'IT WAS FOR FOOD!' – who trembles – it was for something to eat – who strikes with her hands, body, head, 'LET HER GO' – who with a groan lies down on the ground while the car leaves with Kathy, leaves with what remained of her life.

A child curled in a ball is crying surrounded by the dogs. Eyes brush over her in a caress, then disappear.

The epilogue of *Lost* is showing on one hundred screens.

◆ ◆ ◆

Meg throws up on a metal step deep in an alley. In her hands, a pulp of sealed envelopes, bits of paper damp with dried tears.

The stork is beside her, smoking.

'I wanted to give them to you anyway.'

'I don't want to read them anymore, Jesus, it's too much!'

Her voice is trembling.

She wipes her mouth.

'So stop reading them. Save them for later.'

'Later when?'

'Just later.'

'When things get better?' in a quiet voice.

'Exactly. When things get better.'

Silence.

✦ ✦ ✦

'It's for my concert. It's important.'

'Well go practise downstairs. I have a headache.'

'Downstairs?'

In pyjamas, feet in yellow plastic boots, violin in one hand, bow in the other, Roxane goes down the apartment block stairs. A life behind every door, she tells herself. Which one.

It's cold. Opens the door to the basement. Dark. Goes down.

Frozen concrete, piles of stuff, spiderwebs, her old Big Wheel under a mildewed tarp, Roxane pulls it out, sits on it. Puts the score on the floor.

Okay.

Shivers. Sits up straight. Breathes.

Do-do-la-mi-ti ...

And plays.

Sitting on her Big Wheel, in pyjamas, yellow boots on her feet, she plays the violin.

In the dark of the cold foundation of an old decaying apartment block, Roxane plays Vivaldi.

She's happy.

* * *

At the end of an alley, smoothed-out notes:

'Mom, I borrowed your lipstick.'

'Mom, it's my birthday in eight days.'

'Mom, the apartment stinks.'

'Mom, a lady from Youth Protection called. I did like you told me.'

'Mom, do you remember the time I told you to shut up? I'm sorry.'

'Mom, Francis has started wetting the bed again.'

'Mom, I got eight out of ten in math, and I got a good grade in dictation too.'

'Mom, I'm sick. I think I'm going to die.'

* * *

The door to Kevin's bedroom opens slowly. Kevin steps out. The red cape around his shoulders drags on the ground. The apartment is silent. Steve has fallen asleep in the living room. Kevin goes over to him. Looks at his dad. Kevin tentatively moves even closer.

Slowly, he puts his arms around Steve's shoulders, gets on top of him. Then curls up in a little ball against his torso, where he lays his head. He pulls the red cape like a blanket over the two tired bodies. And after making sure his father is properly covered, Kevin falls asleep at his side.

A moment.

Steve gently puts his big arm around his sleeping son's delicate body.

* * *

Midnight. Kicks the Big Wheel back under the tarp. Goes up the cold basement stairs. It was a good practice. She'll be ready for the concert. She walks by the building door. The moon is up. Not many people on the sidewalks. A few prostitutes on the corner.

The wind kicks up the snow. The prostitutes are in their short skirts behind a curtain of snowflakes. They look like they're inside those glass globes you shake, like little elves under fake snow. The neighbour's mother is there. She still recognizes her over her bones.

Roxane would play a concert just for them. A prostitute concert, a concert for lost women by a lost girl. The music would be just for them and would warm everyone up. Even when the music was finished, it would stay in their stomachs, or somewhere close. Like a fire that reminds you that you exist and gets you through the night.

Roxane goes up to bed.

The boys knock on the bathroom door, but Mélissa doesn't answer. They're hungry. They're hot. They smell. They need her so she stays locked in there. She has nothing left to give today. They keep knocking, but Mélissa stays frozen in front of the mirror.

A space suspended in time. As if everything stopped.

Two red fingers. Index and middle finger.

Blood on her fingers.

Small in the large bathroom. The knocking on the door farther and farther away. Blows, muffled cries.

Mélissa is all alone and puts her fingers between her legs.

Red fingers.

Mélissa in the mirror. She pushes back her long hair and finally looks at herself.

Eyes looking into eyes. Fingers at her mouth. Slowly. Paints one lip. Then the other.

Red lips.

Today Mélissa is a woman.

✦ ✦ ✦

People are hurrying along Rue Ontario. Arms filled with packages. Eye level with the bags, Kelly tries to guess what's inside them. Pyjamas. A plant. A book. Chocolate. Sparkly jewellery. A red dress. A bottle of wine. Champagne. Warm sauerkraut. A Christmas tree with lights. A fireplace. Music. Kathy.

A gun.

In the schoolyard, Roxane is talking to Anastasia. She's getting to know everything about her. She sees her more and more often. She feels good when she's with her.

Roxane gets hit on the back of the head.

Doesn't matter. She continues the conversation.

◆ ◆ ◆

In violin class, the students are listening to instructions. The concert is coming up, and the teacher in his white shirt passes around a sheet on which students write the name of their guests. It's Roxane's turn. Mom, Dad … Anastasia.

She has guests, like everyone else. She is like everyone else.

◆ ◆ ◆

Her head is pounding. Even though she didn't drink today.

Louise is sitting at the table, chopping onions. Today she is cooking for her daughter. It's been a while. She can't even remember the last time. Roxane is in her bedroom playing the violin. It sounds like the same note over and over.

Shepherd's pie.

Ouch … It's like cramps in her head; it starts from the middle and goes all the way around. Have to remember how to make it – onions – are there onions? She chops them into small pieces. Her head is pounding. The knife falls, she picks it up, bangs her knee – fuck – everything is so hard – the onions make her cry, she can't see anything, the can of corn, the can opener, what order?

The meat in the freezer – have to take it out – shooting pain in her head – the violin – Christ, that's loud – she doesn't want to shout – she doesn't shout she won't shout – the meat the meat the corn okay the corn – drops the can, it all scatters, yellow all over the floor …

Louise sits down. A weak *fuck* on her lips. Then, head in her hands, cries. Cries for the stupid corn on the floor, the ruined shepherd's pie, the goddamn violin pissing her off – why does it piss her off? – cries for her ugly, ruined life, the smacks she's received, the shit she's eaten, her daughter who's messed up because she's fucked everything up, even the goddamn shepherd's pie …

'Mom?'

Louise is bawling, her head in the onions.

Roxane cleans up the corn from the floor.

Sits beside her mother.

'It's okay, Mom. It's good without corn too …'

'Noooo.'

'Yes, it is …'

Loud sobs move in waves along her back.

Roxane puts her hand over them, rubs her mother's shoulders.

A long pause.

Louise slowly lifts her head, sniffs.

The two women look at each other.

Mirror.

Don't fuck up like me. Don't fuck up.

Roxane stands up, takes the meat out of the freezer, gets out the bag of potatoes, sits across from her mother, hands her a knife.

'First you need potatoes.'

Louise wipes her eyes, pulls a potato toward her, starts peeling it.

Roxane does the same.

Louise and Roxane cut potatoes in silence. Sometimes they lift their heads and look at each other.

✦ ✦ ✦

'Reptile and slow …'

'Turtle! Turtle!'

The real point of the game is to answer with your mouth as full as possible.

'You got it!'

'Yesssssss!'

Watching a crappy game show hosted by a guy who smiles too wide, they eat their shepherd's pie without corn and too much ketchup and it's really good.

✦ ✦ ✦

Salvation Army.

Marc in his small bedroom.

A mickey on his table less than three feet from him – a bitter oasis. Marc closes his eyes. He's hot. He's cold. He takes a deep breath.

The wood cracking, the wind blowing, the comforting fire – the ocean – its smell reaches him. Feeling alive. He misses it all so much.

Don't do it.

Feeling his feet on the ground somewhere, feeling part of the world.

Don't drink, you idiot.

Marc is trembling.

The boat on the window ledge.

Think of his dreams – come on. His house in the woods on the edge of the cliff perched over the proud sea.

Feeling alive.

His entire body, resisting, trembles from desire and crushing fear.

Don't drink.

Don't drink.

✦ ✦ ✦

Roxane holds the phone in both hands, tight, as if she might drop it.

'Hi, Dad?'

'(…)'

'Good. You?'

'(…)'

'You sound tired.'

'(…)'

'Are you moving out of there soon?'

'(…)'

'Oh.'

'(…)'

'Hey, Dad, tomorrow's my concert. You didn't forget, right?'

'(…)'

'Yeah, tomorrow. You'll come, right?'

'(…)'

'Yeah, I can't wait!'

'(…)'

'Lots of pieces.'

'(…)'

'Why now?'

'(…)'

'Okay.'

Roxane puts the phone down on her bed and sets the violin at the base of her neck. She plays for her father.

◆　◆　◆

The violin is nice; maybe one day she will play too. Romantic music or music from some movie about the olden days, where people dance in a big room with big dresses and potential lovers while outside a war is starting. Or something like that. She could ask Roxane to show her the notes. She may be weird, but she's good. She can really play.

Mélissa roots through a big case, takes out some lipstick. Red red red. She likes that one.

'Fuck!'

The lipstick breaks in her hands; she has red grease everywhere. They say it's made with seal blubber … Dying on an ice floe to end up on a girl's lips. Not such a bad fate, really.

She runs her index finger over the red and spreads the colour over her lips. She wishes her lips were thicker. Smutty lips.

They already look better with the red.

Her mother would have wet her finger and wiped away the stuff outside the lines.

But she's not here.

Black now. Around her blue eyes it looks tough. She looks like a rocker.

Her hair is bugging her. She has baby hair. Too soft. They'll never believe her.

She pulls it back. A ponytail. Like her mother.

That's better.

There's no long mirror, so she sees herself only in little bits, detached pieces.

She slowly moves the little mirror over her face. Her big blue eyes are made up with very black black, top and bottom. Her cheeks are pink on her pale face. Her mouth is red and shiny. She looks a bit less like a kid … Anyway, it should be fine in the dark.

She keeps moving the mirror around. She has on her mother's little leather top. And underneath, fake tits. Stuffed with pads. It works.

The skirt is a bit too big, but still sexy. The nylons aren't great; they have runs. But in the dark, no one gives a shit.

Slowly she brings the mirror down to her shoes. It's the black shoes that make it. Shiny. High. Real shoes. Meg's shoes. Her shoes now.

Steve and Kevin are walking side by side. Kevin takes twice as many steps to keep up with his father's. He likes walking beside him.

They get to the pawnshop at the corner.

'Bye, Dad.'

'Bye.'

Steve quickly adjusts his son's toque. Takes out his keys, goes into the store.

Turns on the lights.

Knock knock. Turns around.

Kevin presses his face up against the window, makes a funny face.

'Hey, you're getting my window all dirty!' Steve smiles. 'Get out of here. Scram!'

Kevin takes off running.

The pawnshop window is spotless, and a cleaner is carefully mopping between the piled screens where a hundred times over Superman saves lives that count. He bends over, pulls the plug. Everything goes out.

Steve wrings out the mop with one hand and keeps cleaning.

✦ ✦ ✦

Roxane ties a red scarf around her head. Like Anastasia.

She leaves a few tendrils of hair showing.

Pretty. She thinks she is pretty. Her long dress hangs down to her shoes. She has lengthened her eyelashes with mascara. It's the first time. She has smoothed her short hair with gel and even put on perfume from the little bottle in the bathroom. Pretty. She thinks she is pretty.

She picks up her violin case just to see what she looks like with it. The dress, the shoes, the violin. Roxane smiles.

Has to leave.

Comes out of her room.

The TV is off. She doesn't remember the last time that happened.

The TV is off, and the shower is running. Almost like a normal household.

Her concert is tonight. Her concert.

The TV is off, and the shower is running because her mother is going to come and is getting ready.

Roxane places the picture of Anastasia at the bottom of her violin case.

Ready to go.

The shower is still running.

Opens the door a crack, cloud of warmth: 'Mom, I'm going. I'll save you a seat.'

A meek *yes* from under the water, *see you there*.

Closes the door, goes outside. The wind is whipping up the snow and deposits a white veil on the street. Roxane walks through it. There's no yellow school bus today. She is going to walk to school today. She is playing a concert today.

She knows exactly where she is going today.

◆　◆　◆

It's dark. The air lashes and cars are beeping. It smells like sex and beer.

People are making out and swatting at each other on the brightly lit Main.

It's Friday.

You wonder where they got the number from. Fifty. Can't come within fifty metres of your mother. When you get to forty-nine, does it start to burn? Does she go up in flames? Spontaneously combust?

Fifty. Mélissa has done the calculation.

If she were to lie down on the ground, it would be around thirty times her. And with the heels, it would be a bit less.

The letter crack is empty. Her white papers have flown off into the void of the neighbourhood. Mélissa wonders who will read them.

She's there, on the other side. A car stops in front of the group.

No … don't get in. Wait for me.

Another girl is leaving. Oof.

Okay. I have to walk properly.

Mélissa takes a deep breath.

◆　◆　◆

The chairs are all lined up in the auditorium. It looks nice. It's organized. A few people are already there. Roxane gets up onstage and walks between the music stands. Turns back toward the room; the light hits her as if it recognizes her. In an hour, she is going to play for an audience, for her father, for her mother.

She looks at the room and chooses two seats, the best ones.

She steps down. Writes, concentrating, two 'reserved' signs, which she places on the two best seats in the house. For her parents.

◆　◆　◆

Her heel squeezed in the vise of the shoe, clacking on the sidewalk, the child's foot teeters but stays upright. Clack, another step, she advances, delicately, head held high and brow furrowed. Fifty metres from the other side of the street, she turns slowly toward the group of matchstick women. She is trembling but she is standing tall. Her thighs are shaking, her ankles are tensed, her lips are taut, but her head is high. She looks at her mother.

'Hey, what the fuck, who's she?'

There's raspy squawking from the group: there's competition on the other side of the street.

'Meg, isn't that your girl?'

Meg turns around. Silence.

Her big blue eyes cross the fifty metres. To meet the eyes of the prostitute across the street.

For a moment, Hochelaga is still. There's no more shouting, it doesn't smell, it stops shining everywhere. It's just a dark, biting night where nothing else exists but two sets of eyes meeting.

◆ ◆ ◆

Jesus … like wind between her dry lips.

Louise, standing in front of the mirror. Not moving. Like a ghost. Pale. Hollows of sadness under her eyes.

She looks at herself, and Jesus, is she ever ugly.

She has nothing to hide her face. She stopped using makeup a long time ago. It's been a long time.

She would cry, but there's nothing left.

She would have a drink, but she's decided she should hold off tonight.

She wets her hair. A bit, just with her fingers. Then her whole head under the tap.

She looks at herself. Smiles a fake smile. Starts to laugh. Slams the door.

'Okay, what should I wear?' Nothing fits her anymore. She's gotten fat. A fat ass.

She takes out a skirt. It looks cold outside. Cold wind on her cheeks – it will probably remind her she's alive. She would walk out with her skirt and a nice coat – would say *hello, Mr. Gingras* to the neighbour clearing the snow from his car, *hello, Ms. Vigneault* to her neighbour picking up her mail – then she wouldn't say anything to the prostitutes but she would look at them because it's fucking cold and women have each other's backs.

She would walk like that, at a good clip, to the school. When she gets there, she would smile at people, not even forced. She would say, 'Jesus, it's cold,' the way people do, and the people at the school would say to each other, 'So that's Roxane's mother,' and they would be surprised because she looks like she's got it together, Roxane's mother.

And then she would sit down with the other mothers, the concert would start, and Roxane would be really good, and everyone would say, 'She's good, your daughter is good, madame, she's good!'

And she would say, 'I know.'

◆ ◆ ◆

Mélissa is motionless in front of her mother, each on their side of the street. Smells her scent. Something animal is guiding her steps.

Clack clack on her piece of the sidewalk, Meg heads toward the street.

Hey, don't fuck around, you're going to get arrested if you cross the street.

On the other side, Mélissa in her shoes doesn't fall.

Come over here Mom come over here Mom come over here Mom like a song in her head.

Like a wounded animal, Meg crosses the street without falling either.

Forty-thirty-twenty-ten metres.

In front of her daughter. Looking her in the eye.

A long moment, in silence.

Then words, like a twisted torrent, words of love and hate.

Get out of here for chrissake I love you I've got nothing I'm ugly you're beautiful get the fuck outta here now please move it run – a slap to the face, tears on their cheeks, a hand that hangs on, nails in her skin, don't go, don't leave me …

A scream, FUCK OUTTA HERE!

A child who runs off, flying, feet trapped in a woman's shoes, makeup drawing channels down her face. A broken mother who crumbles inside then crosses back over the fifty metres, crying; like a salmon to its spawning ground she is going back to her life.

◆ ◆ ◆

The skirt is too tight, dammit. She can't get her fat ass in it anymore.

Louise sits down.

The phone rings.

'Hello?'

'(…)'

'Yes, I know, it's okay, I was just leaving!'

'(…)'

'In front? Well, I'll find it if you wrote *reserved* on it.'

'(…)'

'See you soon.'

Hangs up. Collapses on the bed in her underwear.

She has a reserved seat.

She puts on a sweatsuit. It's ugly, but she just has to keep her coat on over it and it won't show. She has to at least put her hair up. Hair up looks good. Roxane must have some elastics.

Her daughter's bedroom door squeaks.

Louise goes in. She hardly ever sets foot in there. Sober, at any rate. It's nice. There are pictures on the walls. Sorts of castles – where on earth is that? It's like Wonderland, with Alice and everything. She looks around. There are pictures, everywhere.

It's covered, floor to ceiling.

Louise sits on her daughter's bed. There's a river stuck right on the door.

It's relaxing, like …

She pulls back the covers of the unmade bed. She should really wash the sheets.

Beside the bed, books, and a box of tampons.

A box of tampons.

Ah.

Louise feels small.

She won't cry.

Slowly, Louise stretches out, face in her daughter's pillow, breathes in her scent.

Pulls the sheets up over her.

◆　◆　◆

Night falls suddenly on the apartment block. On the whole street. Kevin and Steve are side by side at the window. Steve still smells like bleach from his new job, and Kevin likes it. They are looking down at the street together. The car is waiting. Mélissa gets in.

They're just waiting for the third kid, the youngest. They're taking him. He's crying.

'I hope they put them in the same home at least.'

In silence, Steve takes his son's warm hand in his.

♦ ♦ ♦

Mélissa is tired. She doesn't cry. Doesn't yell. She's just tired. Mathieu hid in the closet, under Mom's skirts. They found him anyway.

He's crying. Shh. Shh.

Sitting between her two little brothers in the back seat, she gently strokes them with her fingertips. The car starts.

Along the street, birds.

Mélissa would have liked them to take flight. Here, now, all the girls taking flight at the same time.

The car drives past them. Meg isn't there.

Mélissa's gaze meets the stork's. They look into each other's eyes.

Something like a sigh in her eyes of a child. The stork watches as Mélissa escapes. The stork watches Mélissa taking flight.

♦ ♦ ♦

The violins resonate throughout the room. They are warming up the instruments like little living bodies. From the stage, kids are waving as familiar faces start to come in.

The yellow lights illuminate the space, illuminate Roxane, give her strength. The two seats are still empty, but Roxane does like the others and waves – greets her parents who aren't there yet.

The teacher dressed as a conductor clears his throat and proudly introduces the ensemble.

'Grades 5 and 6 will play for you tonight.'

It's starting.

Not there.

They'll be here.

Can't miss it.

Not both of them.

Lots of snow.

Don't get out much, walk slowly.

They'll be here.

Roxane sits up straight, violin set on her shoulder, eyes staring into the crowd.

Anastasia is there – it's okay it's okay. Roxane holds the bow in her frozen hand.

It's Vivaldi's *Winter*, the two chairs are so empty in the middle of a full row, *Winter*, which Roxane hangs on to like her last life preserver. They're not there.

They didn't come. Roxane, hanging on to her violin, plunges into the storm. She can't play. She doesn't know from where, she doesn't know for whom, around her every note tells the story of snowflakes, slush, and Christmas that never comes, each stroke of the bow makes a winter of ice and lonely bodies rain down on her. Roxane grips her violin tight, too tight.

'You're not playing, Roxane?'

Her teacher in her ear. Roxane stares at the room full of faces cheering on violins other than hers.

'No. I don't play anymore, sir.'

At the end of *Winter*, a string breaks.

The concert loses steam, peters out. They didn't come and Roxane didn't play.

The room applauds. They liked it, shower bravos on the little violinists.

Two chairs that stayed empty.

Roxane cuts through the crowd, flustered. The musicians fall into their parents' arms. A boy in a tie that's too big for him takes a cold carnation from an outstretched loving hand. At the back of the room, a father bends down to tie his daughter's shoelaces. Roxane sees him: he is hiding so he doesn't cry. Because the concert was beautiful. Roxane is hot, everything is blurry; she grips her bow, looks for Anastasia's black eyes – looks for someone.

Roxane opens the door onto winter and runs into it.

The violin, like an extension of her body, stays glued to her hand. Roxane doesn't want to drown.

Red snowflakes fall over Montreal.

The city is bleeding.

◆　◆　◆

The square in front of the pawnshop is empty. There's a piece of cardboard like a tombstone, traces of bodies imprinted on it. Here lived Kathy and Kelly.

Passersby notice a void, but don't know where it comes from.

By tomorrow they'll be used to it.

◆　◆　◆

Roxane heads straight into the cold. Dry squeak of her soles on the snow. The street is empty. As if it were a normal evening. A nothing evening. Only the prostitutes, like ink stains stretching toward the sky, are a small reminder of life. Roxane stops across the street from them. Matchstick women in their glass globe. Long and frail, their black silhouettes are like eyelashes on winter. Ladies of the night, meagre prey. Roxane looks at them. Would have liked to gently shake their glass orb and make thousands of snowflakes dance around them.

Slowly, she brings her violin to her shoulder. She plays in the storm. She plays for them and so she won't die. The notes cross the street. Slowly, they penetrate winter. Then nothing else moves because the music skins the girls on the inside. Because it permeates their entire bodies, over the cold and over all the penises from that month. The crystalline sound of the strings as they're caressed tells them a new story, presses RESET on their inert bodies.

They are motionless, tears in their eyes.

For a moment, there's nowhere else they want to be.

Roxane plays.

Her hand clutches the bow and sends the notes, any notes, into the air. For a long time, because if she stops she will fall.

Her violin alone, in tune, crying out, pierces the emptiness and fills the night.

I'm here. A stranger but alive. Do you hear how alive I am?

She will have to play until she dies so she doesn't go under. Her violin will have to cling to the surface so she doesn't fade away. It has to.

Above the street, through the frost on a dark window, a woman is crying.

Louise emerged when notes crept into her sleep. First she saw the Volga running along the wall and thought she might be dead. The persistent notes split the brick of the apartment block to reach her, and she glanced at the clock on the night table. 10:12 in red. She already knew she had missed it. She just wanted to check. So she got up. Carefully replaced her daughter's blue sheet. She moved closer to the notes on the other side of the window. A warm breath to melt the white film of ice. Down below, on the sidewalk, Roxane was playing music.

The sound was sweet, delicate, heaven-sent. But most importantly it was her. Roxane. Her daughter. Tall and proud. It was her height and grace that particularly astonished Louise. At that precise moment, Louise told herself no. It turns out she hadn't messed everything up.

Now, face pressed to the warmed window, Louise watches her child playing in the snow. The violin is like her. There is nothing more beautiful.

A Conversation with Roxane

The three child characters in *Neighbourhood Watch* – Roxane, Kevin, and Mélissa – are inspired by children Anaïs got to know while working with youth in Hochelaga-Maisonneuve. The character of Roxane is based on the real-life Geneviève Ledoux, with whom Anaïs remains close to this day. I was fortunate enough to be able to talk to Geneviève about her childhood, her reactions to the novel, and her thoughts on the character of Roxane. My thanks to Geneviève for taking the time to speak with me and to her mother for watching young Nathan while she did.

Rhonda Mullins: Tell me a bit about your life today. I understand you're a new mother.
Geneviève Ledoux: Yes, I have a little boy. He'll be turning two soon.

R: What's his name?
G: Nathan.

R: I guess being a mother keeps you busy. Are you up to anything else these days?
G: I just finished studying to work in hospitals in health and hygiene, but with COVID, well, let's just say I'm waiting.

R: Yes, that's unfortunate timing.
G: Yes. We would be the specialists in bacteria and disinfecting. So right now …

R: Tell me a bit about your relationship with Anaïs back then and now. How did you meet?

G: When I was young, I lived in Hochelaga-Maisonneuve, where there are a lot of disadvantaged families, lots of alcohol, drugs, and violence. Dr. Julien* took me under his wing when I was four. Later he told me about Big Brothers Big Sisters, and I thought it would be fun to meet someone new, to have someone to confide in. I was twelve years old and she was in her twenties. There was an immediate connection between us. We were both shy, so we connected right away. She's my role model. She inspired me and helped me a lot. Just like the arts and music did.

She helped me find my way. I'm not sure where I would have ended up. Although I think I would have made it anyway, because I have inner strength. I would have become someone regardless, because I never give up. I'm proud of her and I'm proud of me too. She's my sister, my true sister.

R: What did you think about the novel when it came out, or now?

G: The novel, amazing. It talks about me, but that was okay. Anaïs was always interested in what we were going through. She was always interested, and I'm fascinated by her work, because it's reality. She explains what reality looks like.

It helped me. I was moved. I didn't expect it. I didn't realize my story was worth telling. I've had my up and downs, but I've always kept putting one foot in front of the other. I've never been a quitter. There were drugs and alcohol around, but I never got too caught up in it. It wasn't easy, but I knew I should keep moving forward. I'm happy I did.

She was an inspiration. But I have inner strength. I'm a spiritual person, and I always look for the good in life.

R: When Anaïs speaks of you, it sounds like you are an inspiration to her.

G: Inspiration goes both ways.

R: Who chose the name Roxane for the character?
G: She chose it. It's a character she invented, based on my story. I did feel a connection with Roxane. She is someone who doesn't give up, she is courageous, and Anaïs explains her journey.

R: So, like Roxane, you played the violin?
G: Yes. I've always had an ear for music. Anaïs had a piano in the country, and she would take me there. I was always interested in music. It's an escape, it's calming. I would play the piano, just random notes. She was fascinated by my interest in music.

R: Who got you the violin?
G: Dr. Julien, and my uncle Gaston, on my father's side, got me lessons. I went to music camp. I was very good. I don't play as much now, but I love classical music. The sound of the violin seizes the heart, it touches you. It's my other baby.

I would like to try playing other instruments at some point. I like to explore. I haven't travelled a lot, but it's something that appeals to me. I like to explore the food of other countries, languages of other countries. I was intrigued by Russia when I was young. I wanted to learn the language. I lived with a foster family for a while, and they were Haitian, and I loved the culture. I got to the point where I almost understood Creole. So I love discovering new things.

And nature has always fascinated me. My dad's family is from Gaspésie, and my mother is Indigenous, so I went to camp in Abitibi. And Anaïs would take me to her cottage. I love to be in nature.

I learned to know myself, and I think that's what got me through. I knew I could determine my own life. I have a spiritual bent. I never really got into drugs or alcohol. There was a little voice inside me that told me, 'This isn't your place here.'

R: A little voice is a powerful thing.
G: Yes.

R: The novel came out ten years ago, so how old were you then?

G: Around twenty.

R: **How did it affect you?**
G: I usually read non-fiction. So when I read it, parts of it, it surprised me. It moved me. It spoke to me. I was emotional. I didn't expect it. And her note gave me shivers. When she wrote [in the original foreword]:

> I wrote the first lines of this story a long time ago, after I collided, body and soul, with Hochelaga-Maisonneuve. With its children, mainly, and I felt an urgent need to tell their stories.
>
> The first writings that grew out of this encounter were the genesis for my feature film Le Ring.
>
> Then other storylines appeared, other childhoods, and Je voudrais qu'on m'efface gradually took shape, inspired by the neighbourhood's little fighters.
>
> Because they shed new light on the world. Pure and simple. And, since then, that light has clung to my body.

It gives me shivers. Because it, and [her film] *The Ring*, capture exactly how we lived. How we were truly disadvantaged. How we needed to get out. We were forced to be adults. We didn't have a childhood. Now that I have my own son, I cherish him. I want to give him everything.

R: **The character of Roxane was given a label at school that made things more difficult for her. What was your relationship with school?**
G: I struggled a little at school. No real problems, but I had a hard time concentrating. So it was hard, but it was good too, because it was somewhere to go. It got me out of the house. There were some difficulties, but I always wanted to learn. And I had that inner voice that told me to keep going.

R: **Is there anything else you wanted to talk about?**
G: I just want to congratulate Anaïs on everything she's done. I am

happy that she thought of me for this interview. I recommend everyone read the book. It's a look at reality, and it's important. It can help. We need families and we need love. And when I talk about my past, it's like it liberates me even more.

*Dr. Julien refers to Dr. Gilles Julien, founder of the Dr. Julien Foundation, which offers pediatric care to children living in difficult circumstances, including mind-body therapies such as art and music therapy, mentoring, and medical care.

About the Author and Translator

Named Artist for Peace in 2012, **Anaïs Barbeau-Lavalette** has directed a number of feature-length documentaries, which have received many awards, and three fiction features. Her debut novel in French (now translated as *Neighbourhood Watch*) was made into a film called *The Ring* (2008). Her second fiction feature, *Inch'Allah* (2012), received the FIPRESCI Prize in Berlin, and and *La déesse des mouches à feu* was selected for the Berlin Film Festival. In spring 2021, she will be shooting the feature film *Chien Blanc*, an adaptation of Romain Gary's novel *White Dog*.

She is the author of the travel chronicles *Embrasser Yasser Arafat* (2011), the children's book *Nos héroïnes* (2018), and novels *Je voudrais qu'on m'efface* (2010) and *La femme qui fuit* (Prix des libraires du Québec, Grand Prix de la ville de Montréal, Prix France-Québec, a bestseller of the decade 2010-2020), a major critical and popular success, translated as *Suzanne*.

Rhonda Mullins's translation of *Suzanne* by Anaïs Barbeau-Lavalette was shortlisted for the Best Translated Book Award in 2018 and shortlisted for CBC Canada Reads in 2019. *And the Birds Rained Down*, her 2012 translation of Jocelyne Saucier's *Il pleuvait des oiseaux*, was also a Canada Reads Selection and shortlisted for the Governor General's Literary Award. She received the 2015 Governor General's Literary Award for *Twenty-One Cardinals*, her translation of Jocelyne Saucier's *Les héritiers de la mine*. Rhonda currently lives in Montreal.

Typeset in Adobe Jenson and Belwe.

Printed at the Coach House on bpNichol Lane in Toronto, Ontario, on Zephyr
Antique Laid paper, which was manufactured, acid-free, in Saint-Jérôme, Quebec,
from second-growth forests. This book was printed with vegetable-based ink on a
1973 Heidelberg KORD offset litho press. Its pages were folded on a Baumfolder, gath-
ered by hand, bound on a Sulby Auto-Minabinda, and trimmed on a Polar single-
knife cutter.

Translated by Rhonda Mullins
Edited by Alana Wilcox
Cover design by Natalie Olsen
Cover images © Beatrix Boros and Jovana Rikalo / Stocksy
Translator photo by Owen Egan

Coach House Books
80 bpNichol Lane
Toronto ON M5S 3J4
Canada

416 979 2217
800 367 6360

mail@chbooks.com
www.chbooks.com